HOT AS HELL

AN SSI NOVELLA, #4.5

MONETTE MICHAELS

Hot as Hell, Security Specialists International, Book 4.5

ISBN-13: 978-0-9862730-9-4
ISBN-10: 0-9862730-9-0

E-book version, published March, 2016

Copyright, 2016, Monette Michaels.

Cover art: Copyright, 2015, April Martinez.

Fed up with her incompetent boss, Interpol agent Dawn Wilson accepts a job with Security Specialists International. Her first assignment forces her into close contact with the devastatingly sexy, but far too pushy CIA agent Sam Crocker.

When the SSI team, plus a forced-on-leave Sam, gathers in Aruba to take down a traitor to the United States, Sam soon discovers the beautiful, feisty Dawn's skills are a complete match for his own.

As the fairly low-risk operation goes FUBAR, their attraction ignites and turns hot as hell.

Acknowledgments

No book is written in a vacuum. I count on a small band of very special people to keep me centered and on task. Without these people, I would never have the courage to put my work out there. So, here is where I thank them for taking time from their lives to help me polish my fictional worlds.

Special thanks go to author Cherie Nicholls and Gail Northman for Dawn's British slang.

There are no words that could even begin to express how much I appreciate my primary critique partner, author Cherise Sinclair, for her constructive criticism and unique brand of tough love. So, I'll just say: Thanks, Cheri.

Thanks must also go to my band of beta-readers: Debbie Kline, Valerie Samouillan, and Gail Northman. These ladies are long-time fans and catch all the pesky back story and series logic issues for me.

As always, many thanks to Ezra Solomon, my copy editor. He catches everything the rest of us miss.

Finally, major kudos to April Martinez for another fabulous cover and to Gail Northman (my triple threat!) for putting my manuscript in all the formats I don't know how to do. You ladies rock and make my work look so professional.

TO MY SSI FANS.
WITHOUT YOU SAM WOULD NEVER HAVE FOUND HIS HEA.

"Black as the devil, hot as hell,
pure as an angel, sweet as love."

—Charles Maurice de Talleyrand

CHAPTER 1

February 28th, international airport outside of Belize City

S am Crocker sat in the boarding area, waiting for his flight to Cartagena. Feet propped up on a window ledge, he listened to the rings over his secure satellite phone as he eyed the ground crew fueling a commercial jet. He was tired. He was pissed. Nothing had gone the way he'd planned since leaving the Belizean resort where he'd assisted a Security Specialist International team consisting of Conn Redmond, DJ Poe, and Tweeter Walsh—and Interpol agent Dawn Wilson—on an undercover operation.

Maybe this call would set him on the path toward achieving his goals.

"Redmond." The abrupt voice of his old Marine buddy growled in his ear. Conn, SSI's man in Central and South America, had left Belize immediately after the end of the op.

"Hey, Conn—" Sam kept his voice low and atonal so as to make his conversation more difficult to overhear. The boarding area was crowded and no one seemed to be paying attention to him. But he'd spent too many years in deep cover assignments for the CIA's National Clandestine Service to take a chance someone might listen in, and old habits were hard to break, especially when said habits had kept him alive and mostly whole.

"—it's Sam. Need your help."

"Anything." His buddy's immediate response was a relief. "Whatcha need?"

"To be put in touch with Tweeter Walsh—and Ren Maddox."

For the umpteenth time in the last two and a half days, Sam rubbed a finger over the cheek the petite, but fiery Dawn Wilson had slapped. While the little Brit packed quite a wallop—the redness from the blow had taken hours to fade—it was the emotional impact of meeting her that still bedeviled him. No woman had ever gotten under his skin and lodged herself in his gut the way the little hell cat had. Maybe it was the way she handled a submachine gun like a seasoned Marine or the fact she swore like a sailor. Lord knew, she packed a lot of honor, courage, and strength into her tiny body—and, fuck, what a body. He'd been able to tell she was curvy even through the dark, Goth-like disguise she'd worn. She was a pint-sized package of trouble—trouble he hungered to explore more fully.

Immediately after reporting into his CIA handler, he'd gone on the hunt for Dawn. He'd been one step behind her ever since.

Earlier today, he'd finally tracked Dawn's Interpol Incident Response team to the Belize Defense Force headquarters. There, a man by the name of Ron Lloyd, an officious asshole, refused to tell Sam where Dawn was or relay a message. Every territorial instinct Sam possessed told him the fucker wanted Dawn for himself and saw Sam as competition for the little Brit's sole attention. He was right.

Sam's lips quirked upward as he pictured what his next meeting with Dawn might be like. He planned to storm all her defenses, a tactic guaranteed to ruffle her fur. After which, he would wear the little Brit down until he had her purring like a kitten and cuddling up next to him.

But before he could make a move on Dawn, he had to take care of some unfinished business.

"Why now?" Conn asked. "You need to give Ren time to adjust to you being one of the good guys. Tweeter's post-operation report on Belize will go a long way in helping the situation, but I'm not sure Ren's quite ready to forgive and forget. I know Vanko isn't."

After working deep undercover for so many years, being painted as a bad guy was par for the course. But still, Sam wondered how many times he'd have to tell Maddox that Maddox's wife Keely hadn't been in any danger from him. And, hell, he got shot in the back protecting Petriv's woman Elana. If that wasn't evidence of his being on the side of angels, what was?

"I'll deal with Maddox—and Petriv—when the time comes." Which would probably be sooner rather than later since Sam's current quarry was their common enemy. "I need Tweeter to find out where Syd MacLean is right now and get current intel on the fucker's activities."

Sam's jaw tightened. "I'm going after the bastard and will end him—one way or another."

Syd MacLean or, as the treasonous fucker was now known, Sergio Manuel Lazaro a.k.a. Oraio, had sold his country's secrets and exposed the U.S.'s black ops teams to their enemies. MacLean's drugs and weapons businesses continued to contribute to the deaths of soldiers and innocents worldwide. His latest venture, sex slave trafficking, was just another abomination on top of all the other abominations MacLean had created while seeking wealth and power.

"Didn't the CIA get the intel Tweeter sent to the NSA?" Conn asked.

"Yeah. But while the CIA might believe the evidence that Sergio Manuel Lazaro, a legitimate Brazilian businessman, was the crook Oraio, they didn't want to make the leap that the two were one and the same as Syd MacLean, U.S. traitor. So, after I made my report on Belize, my handler put me on a two-month enforced leave. Said I'd been undercover too long and needed a break ... to rest." Sam blew out a disgusted breath.

"Fucking politicians have no business running intelligence," muttered Conn.

"Amen, brother," Sam said. "Truth is, I've got no physical proof, just circumstantial evidence and my gut. Even with Tweeter and his sister Keely throwing their weight behind my conclusions, the CIA—and Brazil's government—weren't ready to go after a man with Lazaro's kind of money and clout. With concrete proof that Lazaro-Oraio is MacLean, the United States could send in a spec ops team to kidnap the fucking traitor's ass and bring him back to the U.S. to stand trial."

"Hoo-rah." Conn paused. "Okay, I'll see what I can do in getting Ren and Keely to help you. Tweeter's out of the picture for now. He and DJ are getting married in Vegas today."

"Married?" Sam whistled. "Well, I shouldn't be surprised. The sexual vibes coming off those two were as hot as hell. I'll have to send them a wedding gift. Maybe his-and-her handguns?"

Conn snickered. "That should work. You still in Belize?"

"For maybe twenty more minutes. I'm on the next commercial flight to Cartagena and your place. Figured if I went after MacLean that Maddox might bend enough to lend me you as my backup."

Conn chuckled. "If Ren doesn't sign off on it, I'll take some time off and go in with you."

"Thanks, Conn. If we need more boots on the ground, I have some mercs I've worked with who'd love to get a piece of MacLean's ass."

"Bet there's a lot of ex-military who'd help us out if called upon. Need me to pick you up at the airport?" Conn asked.

"No. I arranged for a rental. I should be at your place by dinnertime. Pick a place for a late meal, preferably one with good beer on tap, and I'll buy."

"Sounds good. Safe travels."

"See you soon and"—Sam paused—"thanks, Conn. I'll owe you big time."

"Nah, you won't. *Semper fi*, buddy."

"*Semper fi*, brother." Sam disconnected and leaned back in his chair, a big smile on his face. Thank fuck for the Marine brotherhood.

CHAPTER 2

March 1ˢᵗ, Belize Defense Force Headquarters, Belize City

The Belize Defense Force conference room was filled with Dawn Wilson's fellow Interpol Incident Response team members and the local BDF uniforms and officers who'd worked with them on the joint drug task force. Their goal had been to collect intelligence on the shady Brazilian Oraio in order to find connections to his more legitimate business persona of Sergio Manuel Lazaro and to take out his Belizean drug operations, if possible. Since both objectives had been accomplished, this would be the task force's last meeting.

Dawn sat at the large oval table and barely managed not to utter aloud the uppermost thought in her mind—that Ron Lloyd was an utter twat.

On paper, Ron was the nominal leader of the Interpol team in Belize. Unfortunately, the words intelligence, leader, and Ron didn't belong in the same sentence. A product of mediocre prep schools, Ron had risen to his current level of incompetency through political connections alone. The man didn't understand how to run a law enforcement team, especially one which involved undercover operations and cooperation across international boundaries. Unlike Dawn, he hadn't had any law enforcement training prior to coming to Interpol. He'd studied art history; her studies had been in criminal justice and international politics. Plus, Dawn had two years at Scotland Yard working on drug trafficking cases.

The only "experience" Ron had in the area of illegal drugs was in how to find the ones he used personally.

Even worse, Ron pictured himself as God's gift to women—and had decided she'd be his next conquest, mostly because as the daughter of an earl she had the social connections he desired. His pursuit had begun benignly, then had progressed to irritating and just short of stalker-ish.

Ron could pursue and aspire all he wanted. The only way they'd become a couple would be when a zombie was elected Prime Minister of England.

Dawn snorted softly in disgust. Did the bloody idiot think insulting her on-the-ground decisions during this last op would win her over? Well, his behavior simply proved he was a complete cockwomble.

The Belizean Defense Force liaison wasn't too happy with Ron either since Ron continued to treat the Belizean officer like an indentured servant of the British Empire. Guess Ron hadn't gotten the message the Empire was dead and Belize had been independent for years.

The sound of her name drew her attention.

"…and if Dawn had done her job, we'd have the evidence we need to demand the Brazilians turn over Oraio." Ron glared at her.

Fuck, he's still on that kick?

"But since she didn't," Ron blithely continued, all smug and self-righteous, "we now need to seek cooperation from the bleedin' Yanks—"

"Bloody hell, Ron"—Dawn cut into his harangue—"don't you even read your e-mails?"

Several of her fellow team members smiled at her question. Clearly, they'd read the e-mails headquarters had sent earlier that morning.

Ron frowned. "What do you mean? Of course, I do—um, did."

Clueless and a buffoon—and a liar, even to himself.

"Then you must have skipped the bolded paragraph with the link to the summary of the information Security Specialist International's operative Stuart Walsh gleaned from Oraio's closed computer network. That intelligence plus a detailed preliminary analysis prepared by SSI's Keely Walsh-Maddox for the U.S. intelligence community were provided to Interpol."

Ron's frown turned into a glare. His cheeks flushed with anger or embarrassment or maybe a bit of both.

As Ron opened his mouth to say something she was sure would be defensive as fuck and utterly worthless, she saved herself and everyone else in the room from having to listen to anymore of his inane remarks by cutting him off. "In addition to running a successful intelligence-gathering op in cooperation with SSI—"

Through her sole efforts which he was now complaining about.

"—our team, working in cooperation with our Belizean team members—"

Again, with her coordinating with the Belizeans' law enforcement liaison while Ron perseverated over which agency would get credit for the bust.

"—also shut down a major drug operation. While doing so, we managed to keep the lid on the fact that Oraio's closed computer network was infiltrated. According to intelligence from our people and the U.S.'s NSA, Oraio hasn't a bleeding clue and is still conducting business as usual. We, that's us and the Yanks, know where he is. We simply need to keep an eye on Oraio until the legal types go through the volumes of information collected to see if there is enough information to indict him in any of Interpol's member countries. It's all a matter of time … and patience."

She added mentally—*You'd know this, you odious waste of space, if you had half a functioning brain cell.*

Ron turned toward her, his hands fisted at his side. She imagined she could see steam coming out of his ears. "I have had enough of your disrespect of my authority."

Good, maybe now he'll leave me alone and find some other earl's daughter to harass.

Dawn barely reined in the urge to take the arsehole out at his knees. "I'd respect your authority," she enunciated, "if you weren't such a fucknugget."

Several of her teammates smothered their snickers and the BDF liaison coughed to disguise his laughter.

Ron's whole face was red now, like a two-year-old's throwing a temper tantrum. "Go back to our hotel, milady"—he spat out the honorific as if it were a curse word—"and think about your future with Interpol. If I have anything to say about it, it will be a short one."

What a bloody arse.

Ice-cold rage settled over her. She bet if she blew out a breath, it would be a frosty cloud. She fucking hated petty bureaucrats like Ron who thought their position made them gods. She'd been seriously thinking about quitting Interpol ever since the big bosses had appointed Ron as head of the team for this mission. She despised playing kiss arse to get ahead—and refused to do it. Ron did it all too well. Bleeding bureaucratic crap.

Her thoughts about leaving had become even more attractive after the message she'd received two days ago from SSI's Ren Maddox. He'd thanked her for aiding SSI's operatives and issued a very gracious and tempting offer to come work for his private international security organization.

Since receiving his offer, she'd done some research on SSI. She'd also spoken to SSI operative Vanko Petriv whom she'd known casually when he'd worked for Interpol. She liked what she'd read—and heard—and made the decision to accept the SSI job offer *after* she'd finished her current Interpol assignment which was to take down Oraio-Lazaro's criminal organization.

In fact, just that morning, she'd spoken with her Division Head at Interpol, advising him of her decision and why she'd made it.

Ron's bully-boy pronouncements had merely advanced her timetable.

Dawn gave Ron an evil smile. "Fuck off, Ron. I quit."

She stood and turned to walk out, then paused and looked over her shoulder. "Oh, and I've already filed my report on what happened at the resort, including your refusal to send backup when I and others were in danger from Oraio's men. A copy was in your e-mail box right alongside the e-mail about the SSI intelligence sharing."

The glee on her fellow agents' faces was almost as obvious as the sick expression on Ron's horsey face.

Her smile grew wider as she added, "Also, our superior received compliments about *my* actions from the CIA's National Clandestine Service, the DIA, NSA, and SSI. So, I'm not sure your tenure at Interpol will be much longer than mine … you fucking arsebadger."

On those less than lady-like words, she stalked out of the room and found her way outside into the sunny square that fronted the Belize Defense Force headquarters. For the most part, she felt good, elated that the whole mess with Ron was behind her. Though there was a slight sense of sadness at leaving her Interpol team. Until Ron had come along, she'd really enjoyed her job and her teammates.

After putting on her sunglasses against the bright sunshine reflecting off the square, she pulled her cell phone from her huge tote bag and hit a saved number.

The call was answered by a deeply growled, "Maddox."

Maddox's grumbling tones reminded her of the tall, shaggy-haired, grey-eyed Sam Crocker. Something deep in her core gave a little shimmy. While Crock-of-shit had rubbed her the wrong way, he possessed the kind of yummy voice a woman liked to hear in bed. He also had a very excellent arse and wide shoulders. Large hands. Kissable lips. Abs that could shred—

Stop it.

Okay, so the man was extremely attractive. He'd also been bossy and overprotective and—

A real man ... unlike Ron effin' Lloyd.

Yeah, there was that. Dammit.

"Talk to me or I'll fucking hang up," Maddox said.

Get your head in the game, Dawn. You can fantasize about Crocker's manliness quotient later.

"It's Dawn Wilson, Ren. If your offer of employment is still open, I'd like to accept."

"It is. Welcome aboard."

And there was the difference in working for a private organization—no political haggling. No brown-nosing. No messing around. You're qualified; you're in.

Petriv had told her working for SSI was a dream job for good former intelligence and law enforcement types. Maddox was a straight-shooter. He demanded a lot from his agents on and off the field, gave them a wide spectrum of autonomy in the field, and backed up their decision-making.

Dawn was happy to know she'd met Maddox's high standards and would do her best not to let her new employer ever regret hiring her. Plus she'd earn twice what she made at Interpol. The greater autonomy in the field had attracted her far more than the money.

"You still in Belize?" Maddox asked.

"Yes."

"I have a job for you. I'll arrange a chartered jet to take you to Cartagena. I'm on my way there now. You'll arrive first, so hang around the charter terminal until I get there."

Ignoring the stares and smiles of those passing by her, Dawn grinned and did a little happy dance. No rest for the wicked. Good, she liked to be busy, and the assignment would keep her mind from wandering and thinking about the bossy, sexy, sarcastic, all-too-attractive-on-all-levels-for-his-own-good-and-so-bad-for-her former U.S. Marine. If Ren hadn't offered her an immediate op, she just might have tracked down Crocker and discovered exactly how dominant he was—in bed.

She'd had a long sexual dry spell, and she was thirsty.

"What's the job?" Dawn dragged her mind away from images of her in bed with Crocker. She blamed the sudden intense wave of heat that swept over her on the Belizean weather.

"Did you see Keely's analysis we sent to Interpol?"

"Yes, but I didn't get to read it yet," she said.

"Read it," Ren said. "We're going after the man you know as Sergio Manuel Lazaro or Oraio. We need to get DNA or other conclusive evidence to prove Lazaro-Oraio is Syd MacLean, U.S. traitor, so the United States can extradite him from Brazil."

A Brazilian criminal mastermind was also a U.S. traitor? Intriguing. Sounded as if there would be an interesting story at the bottom of it all. The darker and more twisted the cases, the better she liked them.

"I'd love to take that fucker down whatever his name is." Especially since she was bloody sure SSI would get the job done far ahead of Interpol. She had a moment of regret for her former teammates who were good agents—well, with the exception of Ron. But in the long run, everyone—or at least everyone but Ron—was fighting on the same side and only wanted to put Oraio, or whoever in the hell he was, away.

"See you in Cartagena," she said.

"Try to rest on the flight, Dawn. You'll only be in Cartagena long enough to shop for the right clothes for the op, to be briefed, and to meet your team. See you soon. Out." Ren disconnected.

Right clothes for the op? Hmmm. Could the SSI boss possibly want her to use the eons-old, but highly successful, sexual approach on the operation? Wouldn't be the first time she'd used her feminine attributes for the greater good; probably wouldn't be the last. She wasn't averse to using her sexuality. She'd found that bad men thought with their cocks just as often as good men did.

"Dawn!"

Her arm was grabbed and she was pulled around to face an angry Ron.

"Let go of me." Furious she was caught off guard, she pulled against his hold, but the arsehole merely tightened his grip, tight enough that she'd have bruises.

"No." He dragged her along the sidewalk in the direction of the hotel the Interpol team had used. "We're going to sit down and discuss our future."

"Our future? You nutter, there is no *we* or *our future.*" Dawn dug in her heels, slowing him down.

Ron stopped and shook her. "Come along or I'll throw you over my shoulder. I've had enough of you ignoring me, ignoring our relationship."

The man was a stark raving looby.

"Relationship?" she snarled. "There's no relationship, you arse. I can *not* stand you. I would sooner date the devil himself than you."

Ron's breaths were rapid and harsh as he pulled her toward him. She couldn't get to her gun in her tote bag since he held her dominant arm. With bared teeth, he muttered, "Listen, you bloody, over-privileged bitch…"

Dawn had had enough. She didn't care that a crowd had gathered to watch them. She kneed him in the balls, putting every ounce of force and every bit of training behind the move.

Pain suffused Ron's face as he released her arm and fell to his knees, heaving and gasping as he tried to catch his breath. To make sure she had enough time to get well away from him, she followed up with a knee to his chin, now within easy reach.

"Way to go, dearie," a little white-haired woman shouted. "Bastard deserved it. My hubby went to get a cop. We saw the man assault you."

With Ron on the ground, now rolling and moaning, Dawn made the decision to go straight to the airport and avoid the hotel altogether. She hadn't left anything important in her room, just a change of clothes and some toiletries—all of which were expendable. She had her passport and other I.D., her weapon, and her computer tablet and phone in her tote bag. Plus, Ren had said she'd be shopping for the mission; she could buy whatever else she needed in Cartagena.

Ignoring the crowd that had moved to surround Ron and the little tourist who patted Dawn on the arm, she looked around and spied a taxi dropping off a man at an office building across the square. She turned and smiled at the nice woman. "Thanks, doll, but I've got to run."

Dawn whistled, waved a hand, and shouted, "Taxi."

The cab made a U-turn and pulled up next to the crowd. She got in the back. "Airport, please."

CHAPTER 3

March 1ˢᵗ, MacLean's private island, off the coast of Brazil

"What the fuck happened in Belize?" Syd MacLean addressed Armando Rossi, one of his enforcers. While Armando, a Peruvian, was not as much of a hulking brute as his older brother Alberto a.k.a The Albatross, he was still an intimidating presence with his prominent Cro-Magnon brow, swarthy skin, and shoulders so wide that he'd had to angle his way through the observation room's doorway.

Syd turned his back on Rossi and stared through the one-way mirror at the action in the training room. One of his men was disciplining a sex slave who'd made the grievous error of biting her trainer during fellatio training. Syd should probably stop the man from damaging the merchandise, but he was pissed and had far more important things to worry about. Besides, there were hundreds more homeless young girls on the streets of Rio; he could easily replace one or two.

"I am not exactly sure," Rossi replied, his voice rough from damage done to his larynx during a short sojourn in a Peruvian prison.

Syd turned away from the discipline session and glared at the man. "You're not exactly sure?" he murmured. He raised his hand to rub his face, a nervous habit from his youth, and stopped just in time. He was still healing after major plastic surgery and rubbing the still tender tissue was not a smart idea. The last bandages had been removed less than a month ago. He still had light bruising and swelling.

The surgeon had done a remarkable job. Syd's own mother wouldn't recognize him. Hell, most days he didn't even recognize himself. His cheekbones were higher and sharper. His jaw wider. He now had a cleft on his chin. His eyes were more open, and brown contact lenses covered the light blue-gray of his eyes. He kept his dark hair, but had it styled differently. His genetics had given his skin olive undertones and lots of sun had bronzed him to perfection.

Reining in the need to kill the messenger, he took a few deep breaths. None of the clusterfuck in Belize, however it happened, was Rossi's fault. He needed Rossi. The man was one of the few left in his inner circle who knew Syd's history, from his days in the Defense Intelligence Agency to his role as respectable Brazilian businessman Sergio Manuel Lazaro and as the trafficker Oraio. "What *can* you tell me?"

Whatever had happened, had to be bad news. Syd hadn't heard a word from his right-hand-man O'Riley since February 25th. O'Riley's mission had not only been to choose a new chief hacker for Syd's illicit businesses, but also to have expedited a shipment of cocaine to their Mexican cartel contacts. Those same contacts had called him earlier today and were very displeased at not receiving their drugs. They had clients waiting for the product; a lot of money and loss of face weighed in the balance. Syd had had to arrange for a replacement load of cocaine from one of his contacts in Colombia, at a loss for him.

"There was no sign of O'Riley. My brother and Salazar are dead." Rossi's face darkened and anger flashed in his dark brown eyes. "Your resort has been taken over by the Belizean Defense Forces."

Rossi's anger was understandable—the man had lost a brother, the last of his family—but he had it under control ... for now.

Syd was furious and perplexed; he'd lost valuable men during what should've been a low risk, in-and-out operation.

"*Jefe*," Rossi continued, "there were armed guards all over your resort. The Belizean government has posted signs. They've seized the hotel and the land as spoils of the drug trade."

"Fuck." Syd fisted his hands and turned away from Rossi. He picked up a chair and threw it at the wall beside the one-way mirror. The resounding crash had the man wielding the whip halting and looking back at the one-way mirror, then he shrugged and resumed whipping the young girl. Her piercing screams exacerbated Syd's already raw nerves, so he turned down the sound.

"Where's my cocaine?" he gritted out, a muscle along his jaw pulsing.

"Interpol has it." Rossi swallowed hard. "There was an Interpol team in the village, assisting the Belizeans with the investigation and inventorying the cocaine."

"Fuck!" Syd kicked the chair he'd thrown. Rossi winced, but to his credit, didn't move away. Losing a large shipment of quality cocaine, three of his top men, and a complete fucking resort were problems of epic proportions. "Fucking Interpol. They've been fucking with my businesses for far too long. But how in the hell did they single out that resort to investigate at that particular time?"

Rossi shook his head. "I don't know."

Of course, he didn't.

Had his former employer, the Defense Intelligence Agency, gotten a line on him?

When Syd had run from D.C. months ago, he'd lost his NSA contacts. He'd been relying on the labyrinth of shell companies to cover the true ownership and nature of his illegal business activities as Oraio. That was why he'd had O'Riley set up the hacking competition at his Belizean resort property. A man couldn't play in the shadow world of illegal trafficking without good intelligence. And for that, Syd had needed a top notch hacker.

"What happened to the hackers there for the competition?" Syd asked.

"They were gone."

"Gone where? Did Interpol detain them?"

Rossi shrugged.

Syd shook his head. The man was clueless. While Rossi was a loyal employee, he was muscle just like his brother. Muscle was easy to replace, but, damn, replacing the intelligent, IRA-hardened O'Riley and the wily negotiator Salazar would be more difficult.

He eyed Rossi, who swallowed hard. "Did Interpol take O'Riley into custody? What about the rest of the security team your brother had with him? And my hotel security guards—what have they told the authorities?"

Not that the hotel security personnel knew anything other than their employer was a rich Brazilian businessman, but they might've seen or heard something that would make it necessary to eliminate them as witnesses.

"The rest of my brother's team were also dead." Rossi looked even more grim, if that were possible. "O'Riley hasn't been seen since the night of the 25th when the hacking competition was held."

"Hell." Syd leaned his forehead against the cool glass of the one-way mirror and worked on centering himself. No one in the Belizean government—or Interpol—had yet contacted the agent for the shell company which, on paper, owned the resort. The ownership trail was purposely Byzantine and would take weeks to unravel.

But eventually someone would.

Normally, Salazar would've handled dealing with the questions and issuing statements denying all knowledge of illicit activities.

Whatever had happened to cause the debacle in Belize, the timing sucked. Syd would have to handle the fallout now. It was fucking inconvenient, but what could he do?

But the Belize situation, the missing O'Riley, and Interpol's nuisance investigations would have to wait until he could devote his full attention to them. Right now, he had other business, highly profitable business, that couldn't wait. He was due to leave in two days to meet and complete a transaction with Sheikh Benrabi, an important tribal leader from Yemen, who was buying a shipment of sex slaves.

Besides having sex with very young women, Benrabi liked to gamble. Since Brazil had no casinos, he and Benrabi had agreed to meet in Aruba to finalize the sale and make the exchange. This worked out well for both men since Aruba had banking laws which would allow the money to be transferred to Syd without the scrutiny his Brazilian accounts had drawn from Interpol.

Syd had looked forward to the trip. He deserved a little R&R after all the surgeries and excruciating recovery time. He wanted to fuck women who were attracted to him as a man and not merely to please him in order to escape punishment.

And, like Benrabi, he also liked gambling. For years, Aruba had been one of his favorite places to visit when he wanted to relax, put aside all his deceptions, and just be himself. He'd enjoyed Aruba so much he'd even bought a huge estate there under his Lazaro identity, complete with a yacht and private dock.

"Are you still going to Aruba?" Rossi asked. "Salazar was supposed to go with you."

"Yes. I can't have another business deal go south on top of the Belize fiasco." Bad news spread fast in the shadow world, and until Belize, Oraio's reputation as a reliable provider of drugs, weapons, and slaves had been platinum. "The container ship with the merchandise is already en route to Aruba. Benrabi will want his slaves. He has promised them to his men."

"*Jefe* … Interpol also seized the computer server O'Riley took with him." Rossi frowned. "This could lead to very bad things, yes?"

Well, well, the muscle wasn't as dumb as Syd thought.

"As soon as O'Riley didn't report in on the 25th, I had the techs shut down all connections to that server and had them start to cover our tracks," Syd said.

Even if Interpol, or worse, the NSA, tracked the data back to his legitimate businesses in Brazil, his response would be the same. Rogue employees. No one could prove Sergio Manuel Lazaro had explicit knowledge of what O'Riley and the others had been doing in Belize.

Until he was assured his ass was covered on the computer end, he'd conduct business the old-fashioned way: meeting face-to-face when possible and using untraceable burner phones when not.

"Rossi, you're now my chief enforcer. I want you with me in Aruba. Tell Montero"—Javier Montero, also a member of his inner circle, was normally in charge on the island if Syd, O'Riley, or Salazar weren't around—"he's in charge while I'm gone."

"*Si, jefe.*" Rossi inclined his head.

"Good." Syd angled his head toward the training room where the man cut down the girl's limp, bloody body. "Get rid of the damaged merchandise, but make sure the other slaves-in-training see what happens when they don't apply their lessons properly."

"*Si, jefe.*" Rossi left the room.

Syd exited the observation room and entered another training room. Waiting for his pleasure was his bound, blindfolded, and gagged mistress suspended from the ceiling in a leather swing.

After taking his clothes off, Syd picked up a quirt from a side table and then walked toward the woman. He really needed to release some of his anger over what had happened in Belize.

"Hello, my dove," he said in Brazilian Portuguese, "time to play."

CHAPTER 4

March 2nd, SSI Safe House, Cartagena, Colombia

Conn's right-hand-man Berto strode into the kitchen of the mansion which acted as SSI's base for South and Central America. It also served as a safe house for various allies' intelligence operatives acting in the region.

"Jaime called from the front gate. Ren's here." Berto shot a smirky smile at Sam. "When Ren heard you were here, he started cursing. His Spanish is very fluent."

"Shit. I think I fucked up, buddy." Conn turned to look at Sam. "I didn't tell him you were here. Figured it might be better as a surprise. Guess I was wrong."

Sam waved Conn off. "I don't need you to make this easier on me. We all knew Maddox and Petriv have issues with me." He stood and forcibly relaxed suddenly tense muscles. "I'll meet him outside in the forecourt so if things go to shit, I'll have room to maneuver."

Conn stood. "I'll go with you and make sure things don't get out of hand. We have an op to plan—and the enemy's already on the move. SSI sources in Rio reported that Oraio ... fuck, let's just call him who he is ... that MacLean and Armando Rossi, the brother of the guy DJ killed in Belize, flew out of a private airport three hours ago. The flight plan filed indicated Aruba as their destination."

He and Conn moved into the main hallway that bisected the house from the front to the back where the kitchen and hearth room were located. "Does NSA still have eyes on the container ship that left MacLean's island?"

Satellite photos had showed that as many as one hundred girls had been placed on the ship. Word in the Dark Net was they were to be sold as sex slaves to someone from the Middle East.

"Yeah. It's on a course that would take it just off the coast of Venezuela, so Aruba makes sense." Conn blew out a disgusted breath. "We have to stop MacLean. Selling women, no, not even women … selling young girls is almost as bad as treason."

"I'd say it's worse," Sam muttered.

Sam eyed the front door and took another deep breath, oxygenating his blood for a fight. He'd let Maddox take some swipes. The man had a legitimate beef—his wife had been threatened.

But Sam refused to let it get to the point of any real damage to either one of them. After all, he'd only been doing his job to take out MacLean, a traitor to the United States—and also a danger to SSI.

He exited the house just as a Mercedes SUV pulled up. The driver was Ren Maddox. The front passenger seat held a short blonde woman. He recognized her from the photos in her CIA file. Maddox brought his little wife on an op? What the fuck was wrong with the man?

There was another short person in the backseat that also looked to be female. Had the former Navy SEAL lost his fucking mind? Bringing two women on an op?

Sam had no time to discover who the other woman was because Maddox was suddenly there in his face.

"Crocker!" Maddox yelled. "You motherfucking son of a bitch."

Maddox threw a fist. Sam danced out of the way, just avoiding the punch that would've broken his nose.

Throwing up an arm, Sam blocked the uppercut that followed the jab and used a front kick to give himself some room.

"Ren…" Conn began as he moved to get between the two.

"Get the fuck back, Conn," Maddox snarled as he circled around Sam. "Or consider yourself fired."

"Get back, buddy. Don't risk your job for me," Sam said. "The man wants his pound of flesh." But he didn't intend to make it easy on the man who might eventually become his employer.

"Besides"—he shot an evil grin at Conn—"I have to uphold the honor of all Marines. If I can't go toe-to-toe with a skinny, weakling SEAL, I might as well hang it up."

Maddox growled. "Skinny? Weakling? Fuck you, Crocker. I'll wipe the ground with you."

For several minutes, the two danced around each other, throwing punches and kicks, feeling each other out. The only sounds in the sunny forecourt were harsh breathing and grunts when one or the other of them managed a solid connection.

Sweating, Sam's heart pounding as adrenaline poured into his bloodstream, he just managed to block Maddox's side kick to his junk by grabbing the former SEAL's foot and shoving him away, putting his opponent dangerously off-balance.

But Sam didn't follow up and finish the fight. Maddox needed to get over his anger, needed to exorcize his demons.

Sam knew all about demons, plus he hadn't had a good fight in a while.

"Fuck." Maddox surged to his feet. "Almost had you."

"Not even close." Sam grinned as Maddox switched to Krav Maga, a street-wise form of martial arts developed by the Israelis. The man wanted to get down and dirty, did he? Unfortunately for Maddox, Sam excelled at more than one martial arts form, and Krav Maga played to his strengths. And since Maddox had Sam's service records, the SSI owner was well aware of that fact. The man wanted to work off some steam—and Sam was happy to oblige.

Smiling evilly, Maddox connected with a round kick to Sam's right side. The pain was sharp for a split-second, taking his breath, then dulled.

He barely managed to spin away from Maddox's continuation move of a back hand to Sam's ribs. The blow glanced off him.

Letting out a roar, Sam then flowed into a combination of kicks—side, back, then a high round house kick to Maddox's shoulder.

"Fuck." Maddox rotated the shoulder as he circled back and around. "Good move, jarhead."

Maddox's lips twisted in an evil grin. He moved swiftly forward using a blazing combination of punches, jabs, and kicks. Several connected before Sam, sweat stinging his eyes, caught Maddox's foot once again and upended him. The man landed on his ass with a resounding thud and a loud *oof* coming out of his mouth.

But in the next second, Maddox was back on his feet and on the attack once again.

Sam moved backward, playing defense for the moment, waiting, conserving his energy, until Maddox got tired of pursuing and left Sam an opening to end the battle.

DAWN GOT OUT OF THE back seat and moved to stand beside Keely. "Men!"

Keely turned to look at Dawn and gave a little snort. "Yeah."

They both giggled as they directed their gazes back to the fight. Within minutes of meeting Ren's wife at the Cartagena charter terminal, Dawn quickly realized they shared the same sense of humor and would become fast friends. And after they'd finished a marathon shopping spree in the boutiques of Cartagena, with a not-so-silently suffering Ren as their bag carrier, she'd decided she and Keely were twins separated at birth.

Ren had remarked upon that very thing at lunch when Dawn began to comment on a table of Latino men who eyed her and Keely in a salacious manner. Keely soon joined in by providing commentary of her own, and they proceeded to trade snarky quips about the men's parentage and manners, practically finishing each other's sentences. By the time the men left the restaurant, Ren was chuckling at the women's repartee. Keely then had firmly cemented their new friendship by sharing the most decadent lemon creme cake Dawn had ever eaten.

"You never mentioned that Crock-of-shit was going to be here."

"Crock-of-shit?" Keely asked.

"You had to have been there. He pissed me off." Dawn eyed the man's arse and strongly muscled thighs as he grappled with Ren on the stone-paved driveway. Crocker's strength and grace as he fought had her mouth drying up and her pussy getting wet. She sighed. Now that was a man.

Dawn winced as Ren threw Crocker off him. He landed on the ground—hard—on that so fine arse, followed by a thunk of his head. But he got up quickly.

Good to know, the Marine had a hard head.

"We didn't know Sam would be here." Keely closed her eyes briefly as Ren was shoved into the thick shrubbery. Crocker followed him in.

"So? Why are they fighting?" Dawn frowned. "Please tell me this isn't one of those inter-military rivalries. The Marines versus the Navy."

"Wish it were that stupid." Keely pulled Dawn out of the way as the two men proceeded to expand their fight zone to the whole forecourt. "Sam was undercover for the CIA's

Clandestine Service on a black ops mission to investigate MacLean who worked as a general's aide at the DIA. Sam's cover was as a merc who'd do anything. MacLean hired him to kill me and as many other SSI agents as he could."

"Ahh. I see. Ren's fighting for your honor." Dawn frowned. "But MacCrocker was only doing his job. He'd never kill an innocent. The man might be thick-headed and irritating"— *yeah, protest all you want, you're attracted to the man*—"but he's honorable. Your hubby sounds almost as thick-headed as MacCrocker."

"MacCrocker?" Keely giggled.

"You really had to have been there."

Keely wiggled her fingers in a give-me-more gesture.

Dawn sighed. "He was bossy, insisted on taking the lead in the Belizean jungle when I was the one who knew where DJ and your brother were. Men and their stupid need to be in charge of everything."

"Yeah." Keely bit her lip and muttered "frick-fracking hell" as Ren flew several feet across the breadth of the driveway. "When Tweetie and DJ recommended we make Sam an offer of employment, Ren ranted for almost an hour." She sighed. "It took a blow job and acrobatic sex to get him to stop cursing and to admit that he would've done the same thing Sam had."

Dawn laughed. "Ahh, appealing to the little brain, always a good move." She grimaced as Crocker took a ferocious punch to the gut. A very nice gut it looked to be, but now it would be bruised. "Ouch, now that had to hurt. Shouldn't we stop this? We've got a mission to plan, right?"

"Yeah." Keely looked at her. "I'll grab my man. You grab yours."

"Mine? Crock-of-shit isn't mine."

Keely laughed and threw over her shoulder, "That's not what DJ told me."

Shit! Had she been that obvious?

Dawn shrugged and followed Keely who took advantage of Ren being thrown toward her. She threw herself against her husband's chest and circled his waist with her arms.

Ducking a punch Crocker threw at Ren, Dawn mirrored Keely's moves and then buried her face against Crocker's chest. She took a deep breath and barely held back a moan. He smelled so damn good. All clean male sweat with a hint of a citrus-musk that made her dry mouth water and her girly parts tingle.

Shit, the man hits all my sensory buttons.

"What the fuck? Dawn?" Crocker circled her body with his arms and swung her away from any potential offensive maneuvers from Ren. He ran his hands up and down her body—and didn't that feel bloody good?

"Are you nuts?" He tipped her chin up and looked into her eyes, then rubbed a thumb over her lower lip.

She was sorely tempted to nip the calloused pad then suck it into her mouth, but managed to rein in the insane reaction at the last second.

"No, I'm perfectly sane." *Maybe.* She moved her hands to his chest and shoved. "You can let me go now." *You need to let me go before I start biting and licking you all over.*

God, when had she become such a hussy?

Less than a week ago in a Belizean jungle.

"No." He shifted her to his side and anchored her there with a firm and immovable arm around her waist.

"No? Why in the hell not?" She grasped the arm wrapped around her and tried to pull it off her. No luck. It was like trying to move a lorry with a feather.

"Because…" He muttered an obscenity then exhaled through his nose like an angry bull. "What … the … ever-loving … fuck did you think you were doing diving into the middle of a fight? You could've gotten badly hurt." His arm squeezed her in a convulsive move.

She squeaked, and he immediately loosened his hold, but not enough for her to wiggle away. And she tried. Lord, did she try. His closeness, his heat, his fucking glorious chest were setting her senses aflame. He scared the blooming crap out of her.

"Hold still, little cat. Don't…"

He cuddled her closer—yes, it was a cuddle this time and not a pissed-off squeeze. The man wasn't playing fair at all. How in the hell did he know she loved to be cuddled? Maybe he cuddled all the ladies? And didn't that thought piss her off.

"…move away from me. Now answer the damn question."

"Keely and I were stopping a stupid macho display of hubris." She pinched his hairy forearm—or tried to—the man was solid muscle. No loose skin on his arm at all. So she pulled the hair instead. She really needed to get away from all his far-too-attractive masculinity before she did something stupid and embarrassing.

"Ow!" He glared down at her, his grey eyes flashing silver fire. She angled her head and returned the look. Man, he was so bloody tall. The top of her head hit him mid-chest. "Why are you pulling my arm hair?"

"I'm showing my displeasure at being held captive, Crock-of-shit." She wiggled. "Let go. I don't like it."

Liar, liar, pants on fire.

Okay, so she lied. Yes, Crocker did it for her. He ticked all her boxes on what an ideal man should be. He was *not* a cover model pretty boy. He was one hundred percent man from top to bottom and everywhere in between. She felt a bulge poking at her stomach. The spit dried up in her mouth—again. He was aroused as hell, and just thinking of taking his large cock inside her made her knees weak. She sagged against him for a second, then immediately stiffened her traitorous knees and her resolve.

Yeah, she was attracted—but she was not easy.

Of course you're not, but then you've never met a man like Sam before.

Plus, now was not the time nor the place to explore …
whatever this was between her and the man now rubbing her
side in soothing strokes.

Oh bloody fucking hell, who was she kidding? She wanted
to let him carry her away and stroke her all over—but her new
employer, his wife, Conn, and another man were staring at the two
of them as if she and Crocker were a South American *telenovela*.

"Crocker!" Ren shouted. Keely was clasped to his side as
closely as Crocker held Dawn.

Ren and Crocker were men created in the same crucible of
battle and life experiences. Did women ever have a chance at
fighting off such dominant masculinity?

"Call me Sam." The man holding her so gently now grinned
at the man he'd tried to beat bloody mere minutes ago. Men,
totally illogical creatures. "I think we need to bury the past
seeing that we're evenly matched and are equally burdened
with fool-hardy midgets who'd sacrifice their precious little
bodies to stop us from killing each other."

Ren laughed as he placed a kiss on the top of Keely's head.
"The past was buried once I knew you were CIA."

"You never told me that, big guy." Keely glared at her
husband who said nothing and leaned down to kiss the tip of
her nose.

"Then why were you two idiots fighting?" Dawn asked,
wondering if Sam—and he would always be Sam in her head
now, since thinking of him as Crocker had been her way of
distancing herself, a plan that had been doomed from the
start—would ever want to kiss the tip of her nose.

"It's a guy thing," Ren replied.

"Yeah," Sam agreed with a stupid smirk on his face.

"Well, it's a dumb arse thing," Dawn said.

"What she said," grumbled Keely. "Now, can we go inside
and sit? My feet hurt from all that shopping."

"I can take care of that, sprite." Ren swung his wife into his
arms and carried her into the house.

"Well, little cat, you must've shopped with her, so—"

"MacCrocker, don't you fucking—"

Dawn screeched like a scalded cat as Sam tightened his grip on her waist and placed his other arm under her knees and then swung her up against his chest. She put one arm around his neck and slapped at his chest with the other hand as he followed Ren into the mansion.

Conn who'd stood silently while all the fighting and aftermath played out grinned at her antics.

She scowled at the tall blond Viking look-a-like. "Well, Conn, don't just stand there grinning like a loony. Go get the shopping bags out of the SUV. I've worn this outfit for over twenty-four hours. I need a shower and fresh clothes."

"Gotcha, Dawn. Welcome to SSI-Cartagena." Conn saluted her and moved toward the SUV.

"Want help with the shower?" Sam's eyes sparkled with mischief—and heat.

"No." *Liar.* She gave him her best lady-of-the-manor glare, the one her mother used on maids who hadn't dusted properly or had forgotten to iron the sheets before making the bed.

"You don't know what you're missing, little cat." He stopped in the middle of a grand entrance hall and captured her mouth with his.

Bloody fucking hell, what a kiss it was. This was no gentle, getting-to-know-you peck on the lips, but an all-out sensual assault. Tongue was involved, lots of it, both his and hers. By the time he was through, he'd claimed every bleeding millimeter of her mouth and had her gasping for breath.

"Think about that while you're alone in the shower," he whispered against her mouth.

They made the rest of the trip to join the others in complete silence—his felt smug; hers was full of shock and awe. No man had ever kissed her that way, as if he breathed his soul into her and took hers in return.

She was in deep trouble—bottom of the ocean deep trouble.

Chapter 5

Sam sat at the end of the granite-topped kitchen island and stared at Dawn who'd scrambled away and taken a stool as far from him as possible. She refused to look at him and had energetically engaged Berto in a conversation about the chicken, rice, and bean dish he was preparing for supper.

He could kick his own ass for kissing her in the hallway. It had been too soon. Dawn was attracted; her reaction to the kiss had proven that much—his wasn't the only tongue dueling during the all too brief, but volcanic kiss. Plus, his little cat had defensive skills and wasn't the type to put up with unwanted attentions. So, yeah, she was drawn to him, but, by distancing herself from him, she'd demonstrated she was still not one hundred percent sure about him.

Hell, he couldn't blame her for being cautious. They'd only known each other for a short—but intense—period of time. She'd soon figure out he'd rather cut off his dick than hurt her.

For his part, he'd been blind-sided by his overwhelming reaction to Dawn. She affected him in ways no other woman ever had. When she'd come to him in Belize for help to back up DJ Poe in rescuing Tweeter Walsh, every bit of him—mentally, physically and emotionally—had instantly engaged. It was as if his very soul had connected with hers. That reaction had been why he'd immediately returned to the resort to find her after reporting in to his handler and why he'd vowed to track her down when she hadn't been there.

Fortunately, he hadn't had to wait to track her down—it was as though fate, karma, or plain dumb luck knew they were meant to be together. Now, all he had to do was not blow it. He needed to play it cool. He'd protect her, prove himself worthy of her trust and affection, and then claim her.

Perhaps, Dawn was his reward for all the years of being undercover in the world's worst hell holes, protecting innocents from scum like MacLean.

"Better grab some chow." Conn nudged him. "Ren wants to brief us on the op so we can get some shuteye. We'll be wheel's up at 0500."

"We? As in all of us?" Sam followed his friend to the informal buffet Berto had set up on the counter space next to the stove.

"Yep. All but for Berto," Conn replied. "He runs this place while I'm on ops."

What could the op entail that Ren required two women to be anywhere in the vicinity of MacLean and his perverted buyer? Guess he'd find out soon enough.

After getting his food, Sam went back to his seat and found Keely had taken the one on the other side of him.

"Hey, Sam." She stared at him, a serious expression on her beautiful face. "Thanks for helping my brother and DJ in Belize. DJ told me you and Dawn saved her ass when she went in to rescue Tweetie." She gave him a one-armed hug. "As far as the Walsh family is concerned, you're part of the family now."

Sam didn't know what to say. No one had ever thanked him for doing his job before. His cheeks burned from embarrassment. "Uh…"

"The proper response, MacCrocker, is thank you"—Dawn prompted from the end of the large island—"happy to have been of help."

Sam frowned at Dawn who narrowed her eyes and circled the hand holding her fork in the air as if to say "hurry it up." He turned to Keely and said, "Thank you. Happy to have been of help."

Conn snorted and then coughed as he choked on the food he'd just shoveled into his mouth.

Dawn aimed a wide smile at Sam. "See? I knew you were educable." Then her lips turned down and she muttered, "Unlike some wankstains I know."

"Wankstains?" Keely asked with a giggle.

"Odious wastes of space," Dawn clarified and took a vicious bite of the chicken, rice, and bean-filled tortilla she'd put together.

"Would one of those wastes of space be Ron Lloyd?" Sam growled out. "Was he why you quit Interpol?"

"Yeah. Ron's a proper arsebadger … um—" Dawn looked at Keely and offered a definition, "A painful shit of a person." She then turned her complete attention to her food, effectively closing off any further conversation about Lloyd.

Eventually, Sam would find out exactly what Lloyd had done to force Dawn to quit and just what the man might have been to her. If the asshole had hurt her in any way, well, Sam would be happy to enact some payback on his little cat's behalf.

Once the meal was over and the island cleared, they moved to the adjacent hearth room. A large flat screen over the fireplace was obviously hooked up to a computer which had multiple windows open. One window displayed a real-time satellite image of a container ship flying a Panamanian flag. Another showed a satellite image of a large estate with the latitude and longitude of Aruba. The estate image was also live and depicted signs of active security patrols.

"Is that where MacLean's staying on Aruba?" Sam asked Ren.

"Yeah. His alter ego Lazaro owns it through one of his many holding companies." Ren activated another window which featured a slide-show of MacLean's estate from various angles and altitudes. "As you'll note, he has good security. Comparing the feeds over the last two days, MacLean has brought in more men for his upcoming visit. We have to assume what happened in Belize has put him on alert."

"But not so much that he refused to travel to meet his buyer and complete the sale of the girls." Sam fisted his hands on his thighs.

Something in Sam's voice had Ren eyeing him warily. "Yeah. The fucker seems awfully confident his new identity shields him from the interest of the U.S. intelligence community."

"Which it would've normally, but for the fact Sam intuited Lazaro-Oraio was MacLean," Keely added with a smile for Sam.

His intuition hadn't counted for much with his CIA bosses. It had taken Tweeter's hacking MacLean's system and Keely finding patterns verifying Sam's gut to gain permission from the Defense Intelligence Agency to pursue the traitor into Aruba.

"You don't think the arsehole's concerned about Interpol tracking him? After all, we just shut down his main Central American drug distribution center," Dawn said.

Ren shook his head. "Sorry, Dawn, but no. You and your team did good work, but to a man like MacLean, Interpol's an irritating gnat, one he feels he can swat away and still blithely continue doing business as usual."

"Well, that sucks," muttered Dawn. "I really want to nail this arsehole. If for no other reason, so I can wave my former Interpol ties in his face when he goes down."

"So, what's the plan?" Sam asked Ren, but his gaze was fixed on Dawn's face which showed none of the anger her voice and words had revealed. But the emotions were there; he felt them almost as clearly as he felt his own.

Conn nudged him and handed him an iPad displaying the same views as the large flat screen.

"Dawn and Conn will be doing the close-in work to set up the obtaining of MacLean's DNA. Their job is also to keep MacLean and his buyer occupied while the Dutch military, which will be liaising with us on this op, takes over the container ship and secures MacLean's estate." Ren pulled up a picture of a hawk-nosed Arab wearing traditional robes and headdress. "This is MacLean's buyer…"

Dawn inhaled sharply. Sam saw a look of horror—or recognition?—sweep over her face before she blanked her expression once more. Her body betrayed her, though, as she fisted her hands on her thighs.

There was no doubt in his mind—she knew the Arab. How? When? And why was she afraid of the bastard?

If she didn't come clean, he—or Ren, who'd also noticed the momentary look of fearful recognition—would ask.

"…Sheikh Benrabi. His tribe in Yemen has sworn allegiance to Daesh, better known as ISIS, and its brand of radical Islam. He plans to keep his murdering band of terrorists happy by providing them women. We're fairly certain that wherever Benrabi goes in Aruba, MacLean will be with him until their deal is done. Both men also share a love of gambling, women, and alcohol."

Dawn snorted with disgust. Yeah, there was a past there and not a nice one.

"Dontcha love how some people pervert their religious beliefs for their own interests?" Sam muttered.

Ren nodded. "And that's how we'll get MacLean … through Benrabi and their shared vices."

"Fuck me," Sam bit out. "You're going to use Dawn as bait."

"Yeah, because it'll work." Ren's lips thinned. "Benrabi loves women. All types. But he especially loves upper-class women from Northern European countries. The asshole thinks he's Allah's gift to women."

"Sort of like Ron-the-wanker-Lloyd," muttered Dawn.

Her snarky statement had everyone, but Sam, chuckling. Yeah, Lloyd and Benrabi had both frightened or possibly hurt Dawn in some way. Neither man would ever get a chance to hurt her again, if he could help it.

"I don't like it," Sam said. "There has to be another way to obtain MacLean's DNA without using Dawn as a lure."

"Stuff it, MacCrocker," Dawn snapped out. "Let Ren finish briefing us before you go all Neanderthal."

Ren chuckled. "Sam, there's always a risk, but she'll be wired and monitored remotely at all times. Conn will be nearby anytime she's in the public areas of the resort and casino. They'll have connecting suites."

"I know Sheikh Benrabi," Dawn said. "He'll definitely want to get together and share old times. I know he's fond of Baccarat. If I can get him to play cards, his partner-in-crime will play also. Can we get hotel security to play key positions in the casino? All we'd need would be a waitress to pick up one glass with your boy's saliva all over it. Then I'd play for a bit longer to allay any suspicions, then leave with my newly-met-crush Conn, and we'd be done. Right?"

"Very much what I'd planned, Dawn. Hotel security is already on board to help us. With the Dutch military's help, we'll detain MacLean and Benrabi when they go to meet the container ship to finalize their deal," Ren said. "How do you know Benrabi, Dawn? I need to know if putting you out there will endanger you and Conn."

Sam knew there was a good reason why he wanted to quit the CIA and work for SSI. Ren's concern for his employees proved it.

"I met Benrabi when I was sixteen." Dawn's voice quavered. She took a breath and continued, "My father, the Earl of Oxenham, was ambassador to Yemen. Benrabi attended many functions at the British Embassy, and my mother and I also attended social functions in Yemen. Benrabi was seen everywhere, knew everyone. You couldn't avoid him."

Dawn looked down at her fingers which were clenched in her lap. Taking another deep breath, she relaxed her fingers and gave Ren a crooked smile. "Benrabi was, shall we say, attracted to me. He offered my father money for me. He truly felt he was offering me a great honor to become his seventh, but number one, wife."

"Frick-fracking hell? Really?" Keely's nose scrunched in disgust. "That's … barbaric."

Dawn shrugged. "I agree, but that's their culture. If his pursuit of me had stopped after my father firmly declined the honor, then my father's real mission in that country as part of MI6 might have concluded differently—and things might be different today in Yemen."

"MI6?" Ren arched a brow.

"Yeah, my father was former Special Air Service and then entered *diplomacy*, much like your CIA agents serve in your embassies." She laughed. "Politics and counter-intelligence are so often partners in our violent and highly changeable world."

"So, what happened after your father told him to fuck off?" Sam said. Because something had, something bad enough for her father to abandon an intelligence mission in a volatile part of the world.

"Father was much more polite than that," Dawn said in a wry tone.

"Just fucking tell me what Benrabi did," Sam growled.

Dawn's breath hitched—and for a second or so, he wasn't sure she'd answer. Then she blew out a breathy sigh and stiffened her spine.

"My parents were attending a function at another embassy. I'd stayed home. Benrabi kidnapped me … right out of my bed. Four embassy employees died trying to protect me. I felt so … helpless." Dawn went silent for a second, then continued. Only the strain in her voice revealed how much the recounting affected her. "Father rescued me before anything … bad happened. He then chose me and my mother's safety over his mission."

"Damn right," muttered Sam.

She shot him a grateful look. "We went back to England. Father is still in counter-intelligence and I can't tell you what he does, or I'd have to kill you." Her lips quivered into a small smile at the joking retort. "To sum it up, Benrabi lost me once … he'll remember me as Lady Dawn Wilson and will definitely want to reconnect."

"Fuck, he'll want to try again. Men like that don't like losing and…" Sam shook his head.

"Sam…" Dawn moved to sit next to him on the couch and rubbed his arm. "Ren's plan will work. I'm no longer a young, helpless girl. I'm trained. I'll be armed. I won't let him take me again. Conn, Ren … you … will all be there to back me up. This is the kind of work I do and have been doing for years. Trust me to do my job. I trust you to do yours." She squeezed his arm, then let her hand rest on his forearm.

Okay, trust. She was asking for his and was freely and wholly giving hers. Plus, she'd called him Sam for the first time, a promising overture on her part.

Don't fuck this up, Crocker.

For several seconds, he let Dawn's touch, her scent, her words wash over him as he thought about the plan. Thought about what he knew of MacLean's personality. Thought about how he could never be seen while MacLean was on the resort property because the fucker knew him.

Why had he ever insisted on that face-to-face meeting with old Syd back in D.C.? If he hadn't, he could be the one in the casino with Dawn.

Since Sam couldn't be seen in public with Dawn, he damn well planned on protecting her in private. He'd share her suite. To protect her cover, he could use Conn's room for ingress and egress.

Finally, he muttered, "Fuck, just fuck. It's the only way, isn't it? MacLean normally wouldn't mingle with strangers. He could just as easily arrange for gaming at his estate or a private club and provide all the women and booze Benrabi could want. But he would go out in public and mingle to cater to a valued client, because the Syd I know is a grade A brown-noser."

Shit.

Sam turned to Conn. "She's never out of your sight. Ever."

"Got that." Conn nodded. "Plus, you, Ren, and Keely will have eyes in the sky. Right, Keely?"

"Yes…" Keely answered Conn, but focused on him. "Sam, the DIA reached out to the Dutch who liaised with the resort hotel. We'll have complete access to the resort's security room and will have eyes on all the public areas of the resort, inside and outside. Plus Conn and Dawn will be wired for audio and video and in communication with us at all times."

Sam frowned and looked over at Dawn who appeared totally unconcerned about the op. Was he overreacting? "How will she be wired? It's hot as hell in Aruba."

He didn't even want to think about how little clothing she'd wear—at how many men would ogle her petite curvy body. Shit, he had it bad and wasn't hiding it well at all. Ren had just shot him a curious glance.

"Show him, Dawn?" Keely suggested.

"All of it?" Dawn squeaked. Her calm facade finally cracked. Her blush spread over her face and down onto her neck.

"The necklace and earrings only. The mike, no." Keely laughed. "This isn't an X-rated briefing."

Ren muttered, "Not funny, sprite." Keely's response was to stick her tongue out at her husband.

Sam, Conn, and Berto shared quizzical looks.

"Okay, this necklace," Dawn pulled it out from under her shirt and showed it to all, "and another couple Keely gave me are cameras and will send live video feed to any computer via bluetooth over a satphone connection." She then touched an elaborate earring that cuffed all along the rim and down to her ear lobe. "This is my receiver for audio communications from the team. The mike for live audio feed is a button mike and is, um, elsewhere on my body." She turned a rosy shade of pink. "They're all controlled and relayed via this diamond watch which is a powerful satphone." She tapped her wrist.

"Where elsewhere?" Sam demanded, stuck on the mike and Dawn's obvious loss of composure.

"Oh, for chrissakes." Keely huffed. "Tweeter created a button mike for when I ever got to go out on op again—"

"Which will happen for you as in never," Ren said, a dangerous look in his eye. "Not letting you out of my sight ever again. You always get into trouble."

Keely glared at her husband. "Bite me, big guy. I'd be doing this op, but MacLean knows what I look like."

Ren growled.

Keely snorted. "So, before I was rudely interrupted by Mr. Overly-Cautious, Tweeter created a small mike that I had a jeweler add to one of my nipple rings. Since Dawn has pierced nipples, I gave her one of my extra sets."

Sam almost swallowed his tongue. "Nipple rings?" He couldn't help himself and eyed Dawn's chest. He didn't see any evidence of nipple jewelry. Hell, he couldn't even see the outline of her nipples. She must have on a heavily padded bra. But his imagination could easily fill in the blanks. He forced himself to sit still and not adjust his very painful hard-on.

"Yeah, nipple rings. Get over it, Crock-of-shit."

Hell, she was back to name-calling.

Dawn glowered at the men. "And all of you bleeding perverts stop staring at my chest."

"But it's such a nice chest." Conn winked, a grin on his lips.

Sam elbowed Conn, hard enough to tip his buddy over the arm of the sofa.

Conn laughed and muttered just loudly enough for Sam's ears, "Jealous much?"

"Now that we all know I'll be *thoroughly* protected by technology and by Conn, can we get on with the briefing so I can take a shower and get some sleep?" Dawn asked. "I only managed a nap on the charter here, plus I haven't had any real sleep for almost thirty-six hours. I can operate on cat naps, but I'd like to be totally on my game when I reel Benrabi in. Plus, Oraio—"

"It's MacLean." Sam and Ren said at the same time with similar growls.

She nodded. "—MacLean has to believe I'm dumb arm candy and that requires all my brain cells to be fully rested."

"Not much more to tell," Ren said. "Our mission is to get evidence to prove Oraio and MacLean are one and the same person. We have the full cooperation of the Dutch military, the local law enforcement, and resort security. As for the kidnapped girls, the U.S. military has a forward operating base on Aruba which will back up the Dutch and the Arubans, if needed."

"Good enough," Dawn said. "Whatever the arsehole is called, he's still Oraio the drugs, guns, and human trafficker, and I'd like to see him finally caught. Interpol will never bring the bastard in as long as wanker Ron is running the op on their end."

Sam's lips twisted. He would take it as read that Dawn had never had any kind of relationship with Lloyd outside of working on Interpol missions. The look on her face and tone in her voice did not speak to former-love-interest-gone-bad, but former-boss-as-fuck-up.

"That's the basic plan. We'll adapt, as needed. Get some sleep, people," Ren ordered. "There are files on your tablets on Benrabi, his people, and the layouts of the Aruban resort/ casino and MacLean's estate. Study them on the flight to Aruba tomorrow. Conn and Dawn will take a separate private charter and enter Aruba through regular Customs. The rest of us will fly into the Dutch Air Force base and be met by our Dutch liaison Captain Hoffmann, who has already been fully briefed."

Sam liked how SSI did things and knew as long as Petriv didn't try to kill him when they met—and they'd meet eventually—he'd really like to work for SSI.

CHAPTER 6

Later that night

Dawn rummaged through the massive refrigerator and found some cheese and an open bottle of white wine. If she could find some crackers, she'd have a nice snack.

"Couldn't sleep?" Sam's low, gravelly tones came from behind her.

She turned and found him leaning a shoulder against the door frame. He looked far too attractive in a T-shirt with its sleeves cut out and loose sweat pants that hung low on his hips. The look in his eyes was warm, almost tender, as his gaze swept over her body from her bare feet with the bright pink polish she'd just applied, up her equally bare legs, and over Ren's T-shirt Keely had loaned her to act as a robe, and finally settling on her face.

She was very conscious she wore only a sheer, short nightgown and no knickers underneath the dark cotton. Thank God, the T-shirt covered her to right above her knees. Why hadn't she thrown on some real clothes before she'd come downstairs?

Flustered by his continued scrutiny, she stuttered out, "Y-y-eah." She coughed to clear her suddenly tight throat and then held up the wine bottle. "Want some? I'm having cheese and crackers, if I can find them."

Sam ambled farther into the kitchen. No, ambled was too tame. His movement was more akin to the prowl of a big cat. A big, hungry, stalking cat.

"I'll grab the crackers and some glasses. Sit," he ordered. "You look beat."

"Thanks. A girl always loves to hear she's looking less than her best."

Obviously she didn't move fast enough to suit Sam, because before she'd even gotten her last word out, he swooped, picked her up, and placed her on a stool.

Dawn set the wine bottle onto the island with a distinctive thud, then proceeded to hack slices of cheese off the hunk of white cheddar. It was better than laying into the dictatorial male in the room, who thought he had the right to order her around.

"I think you couldn't be anything else but beautiful..."

And then he goes and says something sweet.

Sam placed two wine glasses and a box of crackers on the island and then sat on the stool next to hers. "...you're just looking a bit tired." Flicking a finger at the soft cotton sleeve of the T-shirt, he frowned. "That's a man's T-shirt, not some nightshirt. Whose is it?" His voice was low and rough like the deep, harsh growl of the leopards she'd heard in the Belizean jungle. "It can't be the asshole Lloyd's, you'd never give that douchebag the time of day. So, little cat, do you have some man back in England, missing his shirt? Missing you in his bed?"

Little cat? At least that was better than little Brit.

Sam's new pet name for her sounded awfully possessive. She'd known he was attracted to her, the kiss in the hallway had conveyed that concept loudly and clearly. He sounded jealous. But how could he be? They barely knew one another.

It happens that way sometimes, Dawn. It did with your parents. Don't tick the large alpha-male off. Answer the man— honestly.

"No ... there's no one." She concentrated on carefully slicing the cheese. Berto had very sharp knives and her hand was shaking. Sam was hell on her nerves. He was everything the men in her past were not. He was a hunky, sex-on-a-stick-hot, uber-macho, dominant male. He liked her snark and gave it back as good as she dealt it out. Most importantly, he didn't seem to be threatened by her skills or intelligence. Yes, he tended to be bossy where her safety was concerned, but his over-protectiveness was an integral part of the whole package.

If she took on a man like Sam, she'd have to accept every aspect of the package. Men, as her so-wise mother had once told her, were not trainable after the age of five, but they might be led.

And she so wanted to take Sam on ... to jump his bones to see if the promise of him was real. But the timing sucked. She didn't need this out-of-control attraction right before an op. Especially a mission in which she had to play a dumb bimbo. She needed to be on her A-game, because shit happened no matter how well thought out the mission was and how much backup an operative had.

"Then whose shirt is it? Was I wrong and it belongs to that asshole Lloyd?" Sam snarled. "He lied to me when I tried to find you after what went down in Belize. Said you were unavailable. You two have a thing?"

"Fuck no." She tossed a piece of cheese at him, hitting his chest. "I can't stand the wanker. Ron had aspirations ... unrealized aspirations. Besides the man wouldn't be caught dead in a T-shirt unless it were a silk Armani."

"Then who in the fuck's shirt is it?" Sam gritted out.

If she didn't satisfy his curiosity, assuage his jealousy, he'd be at her all night for his answer, and she really would like to get some sleep.

Exasperated, she sighed. "It's Ren's. I forgot to buy a robe."

Sam stood, plucked her off the stool, set her gently on her feet, and then stripped the shirt off her before she could protest. He inhaled sharply and ate her up with his hot, sensual gaze. "Nice nightie."

His expression tightened and his nostrils flared. She sensed he was fighting a battle—his fierce need versus her need for rest. He blew out a shuddering breath, then took off his T-shirt with its U.S. Marine logo, pulled it over her head, and helped her pull her arms through the arm holes. "There, that's better."

Struck speechless, Dawn trembled as he smoothed the shirt over her body. The look in his silver-grey eyes was both tender and sexual. His citrus-musk scent had grown stronger as the air around them heated. He dropped his hands from her body and shifted his gaze to the floor, breaking the intense attraction which threatened to consume them both.

This man had control, and that was very sexy indeed.

Sam bent and picked up Ren's shirt. "I'll make sure the boss gets this back." He leaned in and placed a light kiss on her parted lips. Picking her up, he placed her back on the stool and held a piece of cheese to her lips. "Eat."

Dawn ate—and drank the wine from the glass he held to her lips and then from which he took a sip.

For the next few minutes, Sam fed her and shared the wine. All the stress that had served to keep her awake melted away in the cozy cocoon Sam had woven around the two of them. Even the sounds of the ice maker coming on, the hum of the air conditioning, and the distant call of birds from outside the house dimmed as Sam cared for her needs over his.

For only the second time in her life, Dawn was struck dumb by a man … by his actions and words.

The first time had been in a Belizean jungle when she'd met Sam. She'd wandered around the night-time jungle, avoiding O'Riley's security people and worrying about snakes and predatory animals, and not sure she'd find the mysterious Crocker in time to help DJ and Tweeter. And then suddenly Sam had appeared in front of her, sliding out of the undergrowth like a jungle cat. He'd been as impressive then as now, an air of competence and command about him that both impressed and ticked her off. He'd been the ace in the hole the SSI team had needed to win the day.

Sam wasn't a Nancy-boy like most of the men she'd dated. In truth, men—all types—had always been easy for her to handle. She'd grown up with four brothers, was used to the military men who guarded the embassies she'd lived in, and had competed with males in her educational and professional life. But Sam was different than all of those males. He was an outlier of the male species—or, at least, he was for her.

She licked her lips and swallowed hard. Sam's eyes heated until she swore she saw flames in their deep grey depths.

"That did it." His rumbled words shot a frisson of awareness down her spine right before he pulled her into his arms and took her mouth in a heated kiss. Unlike the earlier kiss in the hallway, this one went from zero to the speed of sound instantly. He'd loosened the reins on his desire.

Sam groaned into her mouth and the vibrations traveled throughout her body, sparking every nerve-ending into a higher level of excitation. He stroked her body with calloused fingertips and then slid his large hands under her clothing and grabbed one naked arse-cheek in each hand and squeezed gently.

She moaned and he swallowed the sound—took her breath and then gave her his.

He muttered as he ate at her lips. "Sweet … so … fucking … sweet. I just wanna eat you up." He thrust his tongue into her mouth, engaging hers in a battle for ultimate pleasure. It was a war where neither side lost.

Mewling deep in her throat, she opened wider to his avid, seeking mouth even as she melted against his large, warm body. Rubbing her aching breasts over his tanned, cut chest, she felt the roughness of his dark chest hair through the thin layers of her clothing. Her nipples pebbled and begged to be touched—no, suckled—by this man's marvelously talented lips and tongue.

When Sam moved one of his hands to the aching apex of her thighs, a warning siren in her head wailed. *Red Alert! Mission. Tomorrow. Early departure.*

Bloody buggering hell. She wanted this man—had never wanted another man as much as she wanted Sam right now, right this minute, on the floor, on the counter, or against the bleeding wall.

But the timing sucked.

Mentally whining, Dawn placed her hands on his all-too-inviting chest and gently shoved. Breaking off the kiss, she mumbled against his lips, "Can't do this now."

Sam moved away just enough to look at her. A concerned frown creased his forehead and turned down his luscious lips swollen from their kissing.

She lifted a hand and traced his mouth with the tip of one finger. "So sorry. I want to … really, really want to … but…"

Nodding, he blew out a breath. "Sorry. All my fault. Wrong time. Wrong place. When you licked your lips, I … sorry."

When he pulled even farther away, she smoothed her hands over his shoulders—such broad, strong shoulders—halting him. She wasn't ready to lose his touch, his heat. "Not your fault. Not even the wrong place. If we didn't have to leave so early tomorrow morning, we'd be upstairs, in bed, with me taking you inside me right now."

"Fuck yeah." Sam pulled her lower body against his and held her there with one hand on her arse. With the other, he caressed her back with long, slow strokes. So soothing, but exciting at the same time. "So … I wasn't moving too fast for you?"

"No. I want you…" She inhaled his clean male musk and the light citrus aftershave he used. Moving closer to his chest, she nuzzled the base of his throat and then lightly licked the pulse beating there. "…very much."

Holding her more tightly against him, he inhaled, a harsh sound, almost a groan, and then muttered, "Sweet Jesus …

don't tempt me, little cat. I want you badly. I want to make love to you until my scent and touch are imprinted on you."

Love, he called it making love—not fucking as most men would. Whether his choice of wording was conscious or not, it still struck an emotional chord.

Dawn was elated. Deep in her gut, the same instincts that had kept her alive in dangerous situations over the years and had warned her away from all the wrong types of men told her Sam was "it" for her. So, him describing the sex act as making love was good; it meant he was invested in her more than merely physically.

She rubbed her cheek over his chest, loving how the hair tickled her skin and added to her awareness of him.

"I'd love that. Unfortunately," she yawned so widely her jaw cracked, "I need to finish eating and catch some sleep. If we made love, I know neither one of us would get a wink of sleep."

Brushing a kiss over her hair, Sam smiled. "Yeah. Rain check?"

"Definitely." Stealing a few more seconds of closeness, she rested her head on his chest, breathed him in, and listened to the steady, strong beat of his heart. "Just so you know ... I've been wildly attracted to you ever since I first saw you in the jungle. I want to investigate whatever this is between us." She angled her head until she could see his eyes. "Do you want that, too?"

His grey eyes darkened to molten pewter. "Yeah."

"Good, that's good." She patted his chest. "While I finish eating—and we share another glass of wine—you can tell me all about Sam Crocker, former Marine."

Her Marine.

"Not much to tell." He picked her up by the waist and placed her on the stool, then pulled his stool closer so his knees aligned along the outside of hers. "I was born in—"

While sipping the wine Sam shared with her and eating the crackers and cheese snacks he fed her, she listened to his life story related in his whiskey-smooth baritone. His voice lulled her into a state of drowsiness. She was barely aware of him carrying her to bed and was sure she was dreaming when she was gathered against a hard, warm surface that emitted a slow, rhythmic, soothing *thud, thud, thud.*

When she awoke the next morning, his scent and the remnants of his warmth were imprinted next to her in her bed. She let out a joyous laugh and hugged herself. He'd chastely guarded her the whole night, proving he was a man of honor and had tremendous strength of will. Attributes she'd never consciously looked for in a man, but now realized had been missing in all her previous male acquaintances.

It was the best night's sleep she'd had in years.

CHAPTER 7

11 a.m., March 3rd, Palm Plaza Resort and Casino, Aruba

S am slid onto a bar stool next to Conn. He caught the eye of the bartender and pointed at Conn's almost empty bottle of beer and signaled two more. The bartender grinned and nodded.

Conn turned to face him and frowned. "What the fuck you doin' here?"

"Buying you a beer?" Sam took the dewy bottle of beer and slid the bartender a fifty. "Get me a club sandwich, please, and you can keep the change."

The bartender smiled, "Yes, sir."

Sam waited until the bartender was out of earshot. "According to Ren and Keely, MacLean's just arrived at his estate, so no worries about him catching sight of me for the moment. I'm taking over Dawn-duty for a few hours so you can catch a battle nap before your guard duty this evening."

Conn took a long swallow from the fresh bottle of beer. "I'm not a fucking toddler and don't need a nap. However, I do need to find something to wear. The casino requires a sports coat. I hate fucking sports coats. It's too fucking hot to wear a jacket."

"Hey, look at it this way—" Sam scanned the pool area, looking for Dawn. "You can wear your shoulder holster, a much easier draw than a back or calf rig."

"There is that." Conn took another sip of beer. "She's in the cabana straight across from the bar. Our girl does not like direct sun."

"*My* girl." Sam's narrowed gaze zeroed in on the shelter. Dawn lounged in the shadows, wearing—"What the—that's not a bathing suit. It's just strips of cloth."

Brilliant turquoise-colored fabric criss-crossed her petite curves and covered the essentials and very little else. The bright color set off her porcelain skin and dark hair, drawing all eyes to her, an exotic bloom among common daisies. She was all too desirable—and he wanted to poke the eyes out of every man staring at her.

"You should see the back view. *Your*"—Conn had gotten Sam's not-so-subtle message—"woman must exercise the hell out of her glutes."

Conn chuckled, a low, throaty sound that made Sam want to throat-punch him. "She's been hit on a lot since she claimed that spot about two hours ago."

"Hit on? And you let it happen?" Sam grabbed Conn's arm and pulled his friend around to face him. "You're supposed to protect her."

Conn shrugged Sam's hand off. "Dawn's job is getting noticed so fucking Benrabi hears about the beautiful Lady Wilson holding court by the pool. So get over the territorial shit and get with the program." Conn blew out a harsh breath. "Besides, Dawn has proven she is the queen of letting men down easy while still stroking their egos. Check out this guy." He angled his head at a man, a drink in his hand, currently approaching Dawn's cabana. "Turn on your receiver and listen. She's a pro. Don't fuck this up by underestimating her."

"I'm not going to fuck up the mission." Sam used his smart watch and turned on his ear bud, which had been pre-set to the mission channel. SSI had the best toys.

"Of course you won't fuck up the mission. I meant don't fuck up your budding relationship, asshat." Conn slapped him on the back. "I've never seen you this way over a woman before. She could be the one to put an end to your bachelor days."

Sam grunted. "Could be. Do me a favor and keep your eyes and thoughts off her ass." Conn had been a connoisseur of women's asses since the two men went through boot camp together.

He adjusted the volume for his ear bud through the RF connection on his watch so he could hear Dawn's conversation with the drink-bearing fucker.

"A drink? For me?" There was a little chirrup to Dawn's voice. She sounded like a perky cheerleader on steroids. He might've been the only southern Georgia teenage boy who didn't like cheerleaders. "What a lovely offer. But I'm sorry, I don't accept drinks from men I don't know."

Damn right she doesn't. And if he ever caught her doing so, he'd swat that sweet ass.

"Please, my lady. My employer will be most displeased." The button mike in Dawn's nipple ring clearly picked up the man's words—so clearly that Sam could hear the drink pimp's fear.

Employer? He shot a curious glance at Conn and muttered, "What employer?"

His friend frowned and shook his head.

Dawn turned her gaze toward Sam and Conn just long enough for Sam to realize she had her ear bud switched on and had heard his question. Then she pointedly looked toward a cabana at the corner of the pool, two away from hers.

Shit. He recognized one of the men lurking in the shadows of the cabana—Benrabi. The sheikh sat there and acted as though he owned everything around him including Dawn.

Mine. You fucking perverted asshole.

Dawn then inclined her head toward Benrabi in a regal manner that had to have been learned over a lifetime of dealing with nobility as an earl's daughter.

Turning back to Benrabi's lackey, she said, "Tell Sheikh Benrabi thank you and then convey my most heartfelt regrets." Her tone was kind, but firm.

"Please, my lady ... my master will think I insulted you."

Sam wouldn't have been surprised to see the young man prostrate himself at Dawn's feet.

"He'd be mad at you merely because I refused a drink?" Dawn sounded angry, but not surprised.

Sam liked her angry tone far more than the chipper one she'd used earlier.

"Yes, my lady." The young man bowed his head.

"Tell the Sheikh if he wishes to speak with me about our past acquaintance, I'll have a drink with him at the Baccarat table in the High-Roller's Lounge this evening. Let's say, eight o'clock. Do you think that will make him happier with you?" Before the man could stutter a reply, she added, "And do tell him I don't ever drink alcohol during the heat of the day."

"Yes, of course. Thank you, my lady. Thank you. You are too kind. Too generous. May Allah bless and protect you." The young man bowed his way out of her cabana and headed back to his employer at a trot, the drink in his hand sloshing all over him and the pool deck.

"Good job, little cat," Sam spoke just loudly enough for his microphone to pick up his words.

"As if I'd ever take a drink from a stranger," huffed Dawn under her breath, her head angled away from Benrabi's cabana. "Want to bet there was a date rape drug in it?"

"No bets." Benrabi would've then rushed in to assist his former acquaintance. He'd have taken her away. "There was."

Sam watched Benrabi's errand boy as he poured the beverage into a potted plant in his master's cabana. "You don't drink or eat anything that man tries to pawn off on you."

"Jesus, Sam. I'm not a bleeding idiot." Faking a call, Dawn put her phone to her ear and then glared at him across the expanse of the pool. Her eyes widened and she murmured,

"Nice GQ look, luv. You must've studied up on what the wealthy playboy wears to the pool at a high-end resort."

"Fuck no. Ren loaned me some of his gear," Sam said. "I'm not this guy, sweetheart. Don't get used to it. Jeans, T-shirts, and motorcycle boots are more my speed. You have a problem with that?" Even if she did, it wouldn't stop him from making her his.

"Clothes do not make the man … but they do make an impression. Right now, your attire says large bank balance and a yacht. If you hadn't noticed, you and Conn are attracting a lot of female attention."

Fuck that, there was only one woman he wanted to impress. The woman who'd been ready to make love with him last night. The one who saw him for who he was. For her, he could compromise once in a while and dress to impress her family. God knew, he'd never want to embarrass her in front of her loved ones.

Conn nudged him. "Heads up. Bartender's approaching. Your food … remember?"

"Food?" Dawn leaned forward, still faking a phone conversation. "I'm starving. You going to share?"

Sam turned toward the bartender and slipped him another ten bucks in addition to the previous money he'd given the man. "Make it to go and add another bottle of beer, please."

"Yes, sir." The bartender hurried off.

"Meet you in your suite in five minutes, little cat. You've met your first objective for the day. Time to get out of the heat of the day and rest for tonight."

"Yes, oh bossy one. Just make sure half that sandwich I saw is mine." Dawn began to gather her belongings while juggling the phone. "Breakfast was a long time ago."

"You can have anything of mine you desire," Sam replied.

Dawn giggled. "You implied as much last night."

Conn groaned and, flicking off the microphone located in his watch, muttered under his breath, "Obvious, much?"

Keeping his gaze on Dawn as she stood, Sam gave Conn his middle finger. His friend let out a snort of laughter, then took a sip of beer while also keeping an eye on Dawn. "Hope she's as into you as you are in her."

"She is." Sam grinned.

When Dawn turned her back to them to bend over to pick up something off the ground, Sam's smile disappeared and he almost swallowed his tongue. "Shit, her ass is all but naked."

"My ass is not naked," sniped Dawn.

Shit, he'd forgotten to turn off his microphone the way Conn had.

"Near as." Sam eyed Dawn's glutes and found them to be as Conn had alluded, in excellent shape—round and firm-looking. He knew how soft her skin was since he'd had his hands on her naked butt the evening before.

"Told you." Conn laughed when Sam growled and shot him another finger.

"Dawn, Conn will tail you to your suite," said Sam. "Take a circuitous route. The promise of drinks and Baccarat isn't going to satisfy Benrabi. He'll want your room number. I'll collect the food and head straight up and clear the room before you get there."

"Gee, now why didn't I think of all that?" Dawn tugged on a cover-up with an angry-looking motion as she still juggled the phone. "I think Conn and I can figure out how to lose a tail, MacCrocker."

Damn, he'd pissed her off—but he'd probably do it again. He acknowledged he was an overprotective throwback. She'd either get used to it—or knock him on his ass.

Conn punched him in the arm and mouthed, "Stop fucking up."

"Sorry, Dawn." Sam had definitely never felt this way about any woman before—all worried about her safety and comfort—and so possessive.

Shit, he needed to get his head in gear, or he'd be the reason she got hurt.

"Apology accepted. I'll be browsing the gift shop, Conn. We can head up when you're in position." Dawn sauntered out of the pool area as if she hadn't a care in the world.

A man separated from the shadows of the cabana where Benrabi still sat and followed her into the hotel.

"Shit, I hate it when we're right." Conn stood. "You need the key card for her suite or mine?"

"Nah. Hotel security's second-in-command gave me a master key card earlier when I met with him to go over tonight's security surveillance for Dawn."

"Uh, Sam..." Conn fell silent while the bartender handed Sam the take-out food. After the bartender walked away, he continued, "Let Dawn get some rest."

"What do you mean?" Sam asked, but was afraid he knew what was stuck in Conn's craw.

"I mean, no marathon sex, buddy. She has to be relaxed and sharp, not exhausted."

"Fuck off, Redmond." Sam snarled. How could Conn even think he'd do anything to endanger Dawn?

Because so far today, you've been thinking with your little head, not your big one.

Conn slapped him on the back. "Hey, I know you. You want to mark your territory, even if it's to make an impression on her and no one else. And fuck, man, I'd want to do the same in your place. Just make sure she gets some sleep and that the marks don't show in the dress she'll be wearing. If it's anything like that bathing suit, she'll be showing a lot of skin. Benrabi thinks she's here alone and he has a clear playing field. We don't want him sensing competition and making a crazy play to take her."

"Don't worry. She'll be rested—and unmarked." Sam stomped off, taking the shortest route to the elevators to the suite's floor.

Yeah, he'd be careful when touching Dawn. She had delicate, ivory skin—easily bruised skin. Ordinarily, he liked leaving love marks on a woman he fucked. But Dawn wasn't like his other women; she was *more*. When he and Dawn had sex, it would be making love. So, when it came to claiming her, he expected he'd be finding a more permanent, less physical, means of marking her as his—after the op was over.

For now, he'd feed her, then give her a few orgasms so she could sleep deeply.

In a way, Conn was correct—this afternoon was all about Sam claiming his woman and making sure she knew she was taken.

DAWN TOOK A LONG, MEANDERING route to her suite as Sam had ordered. She sniffed. *Sam!* What was she going to do with the man? Logically, he had to realize she was competent or she wouldn't have been doing undercover work for Interpol. But men like Sam were wired to protect the little woman. He really needed to get over that mind-set if they were to work together.

Two clicks over her ear bud indicated Conn had successfully blocked Benrabi's man and she could head for her room now. She glanced down the long hall and snickered as Benrabi's man tried to maneuver around two maids and their bulky carts. Conn had waded into the melee as if to help, but merely added to the confusion.

Grinning, Dawn slipped into the stairwell and jogged up three flights to the floor one level below hers, then exited the stairs and took the elevator to her floor. Even if Benrabi had people hack into the hotel computer system, hotel security had buried her registration under an alias she'd used on past Interpol ops. None of the hotel staff knew her by sight or name since she'd been checked in before she arrived and had entered the hotel by a back way, escorted by Conn and hotel security before sunrise that morning.

Anyone searching the hotel registry would find seven women with British passports checking in this morning. By the time Benrabi figured out her suite number by process of elimination, the op would be finished.

Intel from the Dutch navy patrolling the area around Aruba, Bonaire, and Curacao was that MacLean's container ship had anchored off the ABC islands in international waters. Until MacLean's people moved to offload the kidnapped women onto Benrabi's yacht or until the container ship entered the three islands' territorial waters, the Dutch military could do nothing but keep an eye on things.

Dawn's exposure to risk on this mission was minimal. She'd been in far more danger during the Interpol operation in Belize, and that had been due to DJ and Tweeter's situation more than hers. Tonight, she would serve merely as a distraction for Benrabi and MacLean.

If there were any danger this evening, it would come from Benrabi after she'd completed her part of the op and left the casino. According to the current plan, Benrabi and MacLean wouldn't be arrested until they moved to complete the transfer of the girls—where they'd find an unwelcome surprise. While Benrabi was still free, he could still try for her.

Unfortunately for Benrabi, she wasn't a young girl any longer. She was a trained undercover agent. She also had backup. Sam would never let anyone hurt her. The more primitive side of her thrilled to the idea of her Marine fighting to protect her. So much for her vaunted need to be treated as an equal team member.

Sam was in her suite, waiting to feed her and, she suspected, to claim her. A shivery awareness traveled over her body and settled between her thighs where it set her clit to pulsing. Her body wanted him—and bloody hell, so did her mind.

Because no matter what they'd said last night over cheese, wine, and conversation, neither of them really wanted to wait to see how good they could be together.

Bottom-line, she wanted the memory of his scent … his taste … and his touch before she had to deal with the dregs of the earth later that evening.

The elevator opened onto her floor. Dawn stepped out and scanned her surroundings by opening her senses, all five plus the survival instinct every undercover operative developed after delving in the muck. If anyone was watching her, other than the security cameras, they weren't triggering her fight-or-flight instincts. Satisfied she was alone, she moved swiftly to her suite, slid her key card in the lock, and then entered.

CHAPTER 8

"What took you so long?" Sam pulled Dawn against his side and shut and double-locked the suite door one-handed. "I was just about to contact Conn."

"Had to lose Benrabi's bully boy." Dawn stood on tiptoe and leaned into him, then brushed her lips over his chin. Angling her head back, she smiled at him. "Hey there, Marine. Where's my food?"

Sam growled, "Hold on, little cat," then he picked her up and kissed her, slipping his tongue inside her mouth and tasting her fully. She tasted like sunshine, sea air, and some fruity flavor that had him hungering for more.

After several seconds, he broke off the kiss and set her back on her feet. It was all he could do not to strip the ridiculous excuse for a swimsuit off her—and take her against the door.

"Does that kiss mean I don't get to eat?" She looked him in the eye, her cheeks flushed from her morning by the pool or from the kiss, he couldn't tell.

"No, food first." He stroked a finger over a high cheek bone. "Then we can revisit the kiss."

"Sounds like a plan." Dawn shed her cover-up, tossing it onto a couch, and moved toward the counter that separated the small upscale kitchen from the main living area of the suite. Her round, tight ass, neatly divided in half with a narrow turquoise strip of fabric, flexed as she walked—an erotic tease that had him hard and aching. And tested his resolve.

"Fuck me," Sam swore under his breath. His cock went from semi-erect to full-on erect in a split-second. "Is that suit even legal?"

"In the Caribbean—it seems to be." She looked over her shoulder and grinned. "This is far more coverage than I've had on some Interpol undercover assignments. One time my team assisted the Marseilles police to shut down a Moroccan drug ring operating out of Southern France beaches and the Marseilles docks. Oh, by the way, those were nude beaches. I had no gun. No knife. No wire. Unlike SSI, Interpol had no cool communication devices like these—" She flicked a finger at her earring containing a powerful receiver.

"That was the true meaning of being naked." Dawn twisted open a bottle of water and took a healthy drink and then sighed. "That's so good. It's hot as hell outside."

As she'd relayed a bit of her past, full-blown fear consumed Sam, turning his insides icy hot like a ring in Dante's hell. North African drug traffickers were some of the most vicious and Marseilles was a cess pool of violence. Dawn could've died—and she talked about the experience as if it were just another day in law enforcement … a walk in the fucking park.

Yeah, sure, logically, he could accept she was in law enforcement, which always entailed the potential of danger, but she'd been working undercover as part of a fricking incident response team, not a highly trained special operations team. He'd intersected with Interpol IRT teams while undercover for the CIA. The incident response teams were mostly made up of desk-jockey analysts and investigative support personnel more akin to crime scene investigators; their job was to assist the local cops, not risk their lives.

While Dawn might've had more advanced training than most IRT members—and thank fuck for that—Sam hadn't been impressed at all with her team in Belize, led by the fucking idiot Lloyd. Dawn had been deep undercover, shit had happened, and she'd received absolutely zero backup from her team.

Again, Sam mentally swore at the image of her working the nude beaches of South France for drug connections and meeting with informants on the rough, seedy docks of Marseilles.

Get your head on straight, dumb ass. She's alive to talk about it, which means she has the skills and instincts to do the job.

If he kept telling himself those salient facts long enough, he might begin to believe them.

Sam took a deep breath and looked at her.

Her big green eyes held understanding, sympathy, as if she'd read his thoughts. "Sam, I made it out. I'm good at what I do."

Yeah, she read him well … too well.

Sam exhaled slowly and focused on shoving the past where it belonged—under old news. The reality was—Interpol was out of the picture. Now Dawn had real backup. SSI employed highly trained men and women who cared about their peers—and protected innocents in the path of danger—while still managing to produce superior results.

But there was one thing he couldn't get out of his head—"No more fucking nude beaches." Well, not unless he was with her … and the beach was one hundred percent private … and they were the only two humans present.

Sam walked toward her. "No more bathing suits that invite men to do this." He took hold of the strips of fabric and ripped them away, leaving her naked but for her nipple rings and her low-heeled sandals. He fisted his hands by his side; if he touched the nipple rings the way he wanted, he'd be taking her on the counter.

"Sam?" Her voice was throaty, both sexy and a little wary. "Why are you so angry about the nude beaches? You weren't around back then. As for the suit, you and Conn were at the pool, nothing bad could happen."

That was for damn sure. As long as he had a breath in his body, he'd never let anything or anyone hurt her if he could prevent it. And that included himself.

"Didn't say my reaction was logical … it just is." He swept a lock of hair off her shoulder with a shaky hand—his hand never shook. He could be out-numbered and under fire by bad-ass tangos, and he had nerves of steel. That was how he knew Dawn was the one; just the thought of her in danger or hurt had him shaking like a green recruit.

He brushed a light kiss where the strap of her swimsuit had left a deep pink indentation on one shoulder. "After I feed you and we revisit that kiss, I plan on making love to you before we take our nap. You down with that?"

Dawn stared at him for several seconds, seconds that had him holding his breath as he waited for her response.

"Why now?" She leaned in and placed a butterfly-soft kiss on the exposed skin in the opening of his shirt. "After our conversation last night, I figured we'd wait until after the op."

The light brush of her lips had him leaking precum and, if possible, getting even harder. He fisted his hands on her bare, lower back and fought for more of his vaunted control. He was a second or so away from lifting her and taking her where they stood. But their first time should be on a bed where he could give her the several orgasms he'd planned before taking his.

"After watching you at the pool … seeing how other men coveted you … every instinct I possess tells me to stake my claim." He blew out a breath. "Neanderthal that I am, I want you going into danger, knowing you belong to me … knowing that I'll be there if you need me, because I protect what's mine."

"Luv, there's very little risk," she said, her voice gentle, filled with a soft emotion that made his heart pound faster. She rubbed the side of her face against his shirt front much like the little cat he'd named her. "But I very much want you to claim me. So, yes, after we eat, we'll definitely be taking that kiss and what follows into the bedroom."

Thank the fucking hell, she wanted him. She'd called him "luv," and the tone of her voice was so sweet and affectionate, he knew she meant everything she'd said.

"Good," he whispered against the side of her neck, then gave it a little lick. God, she tasted so sweet and smelled like the coconuts and lime of whatever sunscreen she'd used with her unique musk underlying it all. He forced himself to stop tasting her, or he'd eat her instead of the sandwich he'd offered to share with her.

"Need to feed you … now." Picking her up by the waist, he set her on a stool. She shivered.

Damn him, she was cold. He took off his shirt and put it on her. He focused on buttoning the shirt and avoided staring at the rosy-brown nipples so sweetly budded and decorated with little gold rings. They were practically begging for his mouth and teeth to pleasure them. His fingers shook and he forced himself to swallow past the desire constricting his throat.

"Sam," she glanced at his hands, a puzzled look in her eyes, "why cover me up? You just got me naked."

"You're cold." He let out a frustrated sigh and admitted his weakness. "And so I won't be tempted to make a meal of you before you eat your sandwich."

"Such a good provider." She ran her fingers through the hair on his chest and then rubbed one of his nipples with her thumb. His cock ached and jerked, demanding immediate relief.

God, please let me maintain control—at least, until I get her off once… or even better, twice.

"What's this?" Dawn's exploration had traveled further

down his torso. She lightly traced the exit wound on his lower abdomen and looked up. Her green eyes glittered fiercely. "Someone shot you in the back?" The words were uttered in a low, angry snarl. "When did it happen? Where? And please tell me the fucker is dead?"

Her unrestrained reaction to his injury made him even hotter for her. She was just as furious on his behalf as he'd been about her past mission risks. Strong women were so damn sexy.

Sam placed a half of the club sandwich in front of her and then moved to the refrigerator to get her a juice. "Eat. And I'll tell you the story of how I got the wound and first became involved with the traitor MacLean and SSI."

"I've heard bits and pieces of that story. But I do want to hear your side." Dawn's gaze was fully fixed on him as she took little bites of the triple-decker sandwich.

Fuck, she was a cute little thing, so petite all over. Her mouth couldn't even stretch far enough to get around the thickness of the sandwich. Then his brain went straight into the gutter as he pictured her on her knees with that same mouth stretching to take in his dick.

The sooner he told his story, the sooner he'd find out if she was amenable to making his fantasy happen. But only after he took care of her first. Ladies always went first.

"I was in deep cover for the CIA's National Clandestine Service. My job…"

———

"WELL…" DAWN DAINTILY WIPED HER hands and lips on the napkin Sam had unearthed from somewhere in the kitchen. She frowned. "Do you really think you'll have to fight Vanko? I mean…"

"Sweetheart," Sam leaned in and licked the corner of her mouth, "you missed a crumb."

"You're deflecting." She jabbed him in the chest with a surprisingly strong finger. "Fight. Vanko. Really?"

"It's a guy thing." He shrugged, a slight twist to his lips. "We'll both feel as if honor has been served after it's over. Plus, *if* I give my notice to the CIA, I'd like to work for SSI. Clearing the air with Petriv would become essential for a good working relationship with the other operatives. If Petriv and Maddox accept me, so will the others."

Her throat tightened at the thought that he'd even consider continuing to work for the black ops portion of the CIA. She knew more than most about the dangers covert operatives were exposed to. If this attraction between her and Sam proceeded the way she suspected, she didn't want him risking his life in third-world hell holes without her there to back him up.

So, task one after MacLean and Benrabi were taken down, she'd work on convincing Sam to quit the Agency and join SSI. Her second task would then be to speak with Keely and Vanko's wife Elana about what the SSI women could do to stop any future fights between Sam and other SSI operatives over a long-dead mission he'd undertaken in good faith and discharged honorably.

"Dawn, you *will* stay out of this." Sam tweaked her chin. "I mean it. Let me and Petriv handle it our way." He took her mouth in a deep kiss, then released her just as she'd opened to engage his tongue. "And I'll give my notice to the CIA once MacLean is either dead or in the DIA's custody."

"Do you read minds?" She sniffed, suddenly wary at how easily he read her. It was scary to think she might not be able to keep her thoughts from him. A girl had a right to keep some things secret. Not that she'd purposely hide anything important, but still—

"Just yours," he husked in a loving tone that gave her goosebumps. "Just as you easily read mine. You want anything else to eat?"

"No. I didn't even eat all that." She looked ruefully at the half sandwich of which she normally would've made into three meals.

"Good." He scooped her off the stool and carried her to the suite's master bedroom.

She twined her arms around his neck and enjoyed being held against his warm, bare chest.

The bed was turned down invitingly, a couple of wrapped pieces of candy lying on the pristine white pillows—which was odd. It hadn't been that way when she'd left the suite.

"Did you turn the bed down?" She rested her head on Sam's tanned, bare shoulder. He smelled so good.

"Nope." He looked at the bed, his brow creased. "It wasn't like that before?"

"No." She bit her lower lip. "I put the Do Not Disturb sign on the door. No maid should've entered."

Sam set her down. Placing a hand on her back, he nudged her toward the main room. "Go next door to Conn's suite. Use the connecting door, it's unlocked. He might be napping. Call to him from the doorway." He tipped up her face so their gazes met. "Don't, under any circumstances, get too close. He's deadly when he's coming awake from a battle nap. Understand?"

"Yes." She nodded and wondered if she'd have to worry about him.

In tune with her as always, he kissed her lightly. "It'll be different with us, sweetheart. I know your scent, feel you under my skin. You'll never be in any danger from me. Understood?"

"Yes." She understood—he was her mate. They belonged to one another. Why had it happened? She didn't bleeding know. But one thing she did know—he was sending her away from perceived danger.

Like hell. She dug her heels into the carpet and refused to budge when he gave her another light push toward the main room.

Her lips firmed. "I'm not leaving you."

While most people would find simple reasons for the turned-down bed, neither one of them thought it was innocuous. Their shared conclusion said something about their shared perception of the world in which they lived. Yeah, they were meant for one another, would be good partners as long as her man learned that she needed to be by his side, danger or not.

"Sweetheart—" Her macho-man heaved an exasperated sigh. "I'm not investigating until you move back—as in the next suite back."

She didn't move, just stubbornly planted her feet still in her jeweled sandals and crossed her arms over her chest covered only in Sam's shirt.

"Jesus—" Sam shook his head as he tapped his smart watch to activate the SSI communication system. "Ren? Someone's been in Dawn's bedroom. Can you check the hotel security feed for the hallway outside her room? Whoever was here had to have entered after she left the room this morning at—" He turned to her and frowned since she still hadn't moved.

Dawn held his gaze as she tapped her watch and activated her com unit. "Ren, I left the suite at 9:30. Sam and I returned here shortly after noon." She then glared at her soon-to-be lover. "I'm not leaving you."

Ren laughed. "Problem enforcing orders, buddy?"

"Yeah, she's mule-headed. Don't laugh. You have one just like her."

"Yeah, I do. Best thing that ever happened to me," Ren replied. "Why do you think someone's been in her room?"

"The room isn't as I left it—" Dawn refused to let the male bonding continue at her and Keely's expense.

Sam cut her off before she could add anything. "I want to examine the area to make sure there's nothing that might blow up in our faces. Either you or security get back to me ASAP."

"Got it. Stay safe. Dawn, if Sam tells you to vacate—" Ren paused, then heaved a sigh. "At least give it due consideration, okay?"

"I will." She swept her hand up and down Sam's tense back. "But I'll probably drag his arse with me."

Ren was laughing as he cut off the transmission from his side. The audio from their side was still transmitting, so hotel security, Keely, Ren, and Conn could hear what was happening.

Dawn moved to the other side of the bed and got down on all fours and looked underneath. "I don't see anything obvious over here. No wires or anything looking like a bomb."

"Dawn, what the fuck? Get back over here. Now."

Her Marine was past pissed and well into coldly furious. Tough.

"No. If you're staying, I'm staying—and helping." If Sam wanted her gone, he could go with her and let the locals handle the search of her room.

Sam was there in an instant to swing her into his arms. "You're outta here. I'll clear the fucking room." He carried her into the living area, placed her on the couch, and covered her with a fluffy throw.

"Bloody cave man."

"Where you're concerned, I am." Sam bent over her, his arms caging her body on the sofa. "Stay here."

She moved her face close enough to his that their noses touched. "Fine. But if I wasn't bare-arsed under your shirt and Conn, and probably bloody hotel security, weren't already on their way here, I'd be clearing that bedroom with you. Got it?"

Sam snarled, "Little cat, don't…"

A loud knock on the door and a key card being used cut off whatever macho-male pronouncement might've come out of Sam's mouth. He straightened, placed his body between her and the suite entrance, and had his weapon aimed at the opening door.

"It's me. Don't shoot." Conn's voice shouted. "I've got Theo Van Thiel, head of resort security, with me."

"Come in." Sam looked over his shoulder and glowered, his look highly possessive. "Stay under that blanket, little cat."

Dawn bristled like an angry kitten, but she decided not to move since Sam seemed to be in an elevated state of dominant maleness. In her experience, such a state often led to temporary insanity.

Conn and Theo entered. Theo, a tall Dutchman with brown hair and green eyes, had been the man who'd brought her and Conn into the hotel through the back way earlier that day.

"Hi, guys." Dawn peeked around Sam's body and smiled at them. Then she sighed with exasperation as Sam moved to block the men's view. "Stop hovering, luv. Why don't you go check the room?"

"Giving me orders, little cat?" Sam's lips twisted in a brief smile. She nodded. "I don't scare you at all, do I?" he asked.

"Not a bit." She winked.

Sam looked at Conn and Theo. "She does not move. I want to check out the bed. I think I saw a lump under the bedspread."

"Really?" Dawn glared at Sam's naked back as he strode toward the bedroom. His back was strongly muscled with the scars of the warrior he had been and was. But it was his arse that was a work of art. She wanted to grab his arse cheeks and knead and squeeze them.

Conn and Theo came to stand behind the sofa, distracting her from her prurient thoughts. Both men examined her as if looking for damage.

"I'm fine. Nothing happened." She shrugged. "Sam snatched me up and out of the room before I could start searching."

A muffled shot came from the bedroom. Dawn jumped and couldn't hold back a gasp. Conn and Theo turned as one, their weapons in their hands, pointed at the bedroom. And just as Sam had earlier, they placed their bodies between her and any potential danger.

"Sam!" Throwing off the blanket, she jumped up and skirted the men's bodies, and headed for the bedroom. "Sam—!"

Sam walked out of the bedroom, a dead snake dangling from one hand, his weapon in the other.

Dawn stopped dead in her tracks. "A s-s-s-snake?" she stuttered.

With weak knees and shaky legs, she backed away until she reached the couch and then collapsed on the cushions and pulled the blanket around her. She fucking hated snakes, was scared to death of the slithery, fanged creatures. She'd rather face down a band of brain-eating zombies than a single snake. Going to find Sam in the Belizean jungle had taken every ounce of courage she'd possessed—and she still had nightmares about that night. But she'd done it since there had been no other choice at the time.

"Dawn?" Sam threw the snake onto the kitchen bar counter and then came to her. He picked her up and then sat on the couch, placing her on his lap. "You went white all of a sudden. You okay?"

"Was it poisonous?" Her teeth chattered, but she couldn't help it. She buried her face against his neck and inhaled his unique male musk. His smell calmed her as did the hand he rubbed up and down her back.

"Yeah." Sam's voice promised murder for the person who'd placed it in her bed. He rubbed his stubbled cheek over her hair. "*Meneer* Van Thiel, tell me you got a clear picture of the fucker who entered her room."

"Yes." Theo turned his attention to her. "Lady Wilson, I am sorry you had a scare." The Dutchman held up a computer tablet. "*Meneer* Crocker. Lady Wilson. Do either of you recognize this man?"

"Call me Sam, please." Sam reached for the tablet.

"And I am Theo." Theo handed the tablet to Sam.

Sam cursed under his breath. "Fuck me. The mother-fucking, pecker-headed douchebag."

Dawn blinked and focused on the image. "That's Ron Lloyd."

"Who's Ron Lloyd?" Conn asked.

"He's an Interpol agent I had the misfortune to work with." She looked at the tablet again, making sure her eyes hadn't played tricks on her, then turned her gaze toward Sam. "What in the bleeding fucking hell is that fucking wanker doing here?"

Sam's eyes blazed with anger. "Don't know. We'll find the fucker and ask him."

Dawn had a fairly good idea of what Sam's method of questioning would involve. Ron would end up bloody and bruised. The mental image made her happy.

"Yeah, we'll ask him." Then she shuddered. "I'm extremely grateful you found the snake and not me. I hate snakes … they're my only real phobia. The arsehole knew that. Bloody buggering twat. I'll kick his fucking arse and then feed him the bloody snake."

Theo coughed back a laugh. Yeah, she swore like a trooper, to the despair of her mother.

Sam hugged her. "Happy to kill any and all snakes for you."

"Thanks, luv." She laid her head on his shoulder.

"Who is this Lloyd person?" said Theo, a frown on his handsome face. "Is he part of the human trafficking operation with the Sheikh and the MacLean person you're making contact with in my casino?"

"Ron Lloyd was assigned to an Interpol Incident Response team that Dawn was also assigned to." Sam frowned. "He's not part of our current operation. He could've been hired to kill her, but it could also be personal. Obviously, he's a threat to Dawn. Also, he could endanger our mission if MacLean recognizes him as Interpol, since that agency—and Lloyd's team—had been investigating him for drug trafficking."

Theo's face grew dark with concern. "I will have my people and the military officers liaised to this operation look for this Lloyd and hold him for the police."

"Thanks, Theo. That will be very helpful," said Dawn. "You should coordinate your search for Ron with Keely Walsh-Maddox."

"I met Keely earlier when she came by with her husband to view our security room. She appears to be a very competent computer specialist," Theo said.

Dawn had to laugh. "Very competent" was an understatement. Keely was one of the brightest of the bright in computer investigation and security in the world. "Yes, she is. I'm sure she has facial recognition software she can share with you that will make the hunt go more quickly."

Theo smiled. "Keely's already monitoring our system from the estate where she is staying. It will be just a matter of letting her know that this person is present and needs to be found. She has already found two fugitives on the Interpol most-wanted list. The national police have already arrested them. I have no doubt if this Lloyd person is somewhere within range of our security cameras she will find him. If not, my men or the Dutch marines will locate him." Theo paused, then asked, "Can you assure me he is not a direct danger to the resort guests?"

"He's not." Dawn rested her head on Sam's shoulder. "But, as Sam said, this is most likely a personal vendetta on Lloyd's part. He's just a sore loser."

"Ahh, a bet?" Theo nodded. "He lost money to you? He wants to kill you for this?"

"No, he lost *me*." When Sam stiffened, she petted his chest. "Although I'll point out, Lloyd never really had me. His ego was over-inflated. I couldn't stand the self-important twat."

"Such language, Lady Wilson," murmured Sam with a chuckle. "Guess I don't have to kill him, then—just hold him so you can feed him the snake."

"What a good partner you are." Dawn kissed his cheek, then looked at the large Dutchman. "Theo? Can we get another set of suites, please? I'm not sure I can sleep in that bed now."

"Certainly, Lady Wilson. Give me a moment and we'll have you moved."

"Thanks, and, Theo, call me Dawn."

The Dutchman nodded. "Dawn, it is." He moved away and began talking into a walkie-talkie.

With Conn examining the dead snake and Theo occupied, Dawn turned her face into Sam's neck and mumbled against his skin. "Once we're relocated, I want a cup of tea with some whiskey in it, the sex you promised me, a short nap, and then a shower—sex optional. In that order. Doable?"

"Very doable." Sam kissed her forehead. The light touch of his lips gave her a shivery feeling. "We'll get the bastard. We'll get all the bastards."

"I know. I'll even let you beat on Lloyd *and* feed him the snake while I watch." She shuddered. "I don't want to touch the wanker or the snake."

"Thank you, sweetheart. You're a good partner, too."

CHAPTER 9

Twenty minutes later, Dawn settled onto the king-size bed with a cup of whiskey-laced tea and watched as Sam paced the width of the new suite's bedroom wearing only his boxer briefs, his phone to his ear. The view was awe-inspiring. He looked like a living, breathing Greek god. A pissed-off Greek god.

"What the fuck, Conn?" Sam paused and ran agitated fingers through his hair. "Lloyd has to have entered—and left—the resort grounds somewhere. He was here. He could still be here. Find him. He's not the invisible-fucking-man, for chrissakes."

Sam turned to look at her and the frustration and anger on his face was almost palpable. "He couldn't possibly manage to avoid all the resort's security cameras. Hell, I walked the fucking grounds this morning and missed locating half of them, and I knew they were there because I'd seen the feeds in the security room."

Dawn sipped her doctored tea and let the warmth sweep away the chill which had settled in her stomach when she'd seen the snake left in her bed.

Lloyd had always been a pain in her arse, but she hadn't ever expected him to try to kill her. Stalk her? Yes. Drive her up a frigging wall? Yes. Sexually attack her? Probably.

End her and end his chance, remote as it was, of marrying minor royalty? No.

"...agree. He still has to be on the grounds. He's blending in somehow, maybe dressed as a resort employee. Any security officers watching the feed need to watch for a man purposely avoiding the visible cameras. Also, has Keely run her facial identity software against the feed for the last few hours?" Sam grunted. "Okay, good. I know Keely's the best. And I trust you, man. I just don't want him anywhere near Dawn while she's occupied with MacLean and Benrabi."

Sam stared at her. Slowly, she let the comforter slip down to just above her breasts. His face grew less grim as his suddenly hot gaze roamed over her naked shoulders and cleavage. She lowered the cover and flashed him a naked breast. He smiled and shook his head at her teasing move.

"Thanks, Conn. I'll stay with Dawn until around 1800 hours, then leave through the connecting door to your suite and head up to the casino security room to get set up for the op. With luck, we'll get the DNA we need from MacLean as soon as he sits down. Once that happens, Dawn's out of it. She and Keely can monitor the cleanup from the safety of the estate."

Sam exhaled. "Yeah, she's too good for me. I'm a lucky guy. Later." He swiped off his phone which he tossed onto a chaise.

Too good for him? Where in the bleeding hell had that come from?

"Maybe I think I'm the lucky one." Dawn had never met a man who looked like Sam, and had his warrior background, with such low self-esteem. Most men with his bona fides were arrogant arseholes.

"Little cat—" The endearment spoken in his husky baritone warmed her from the inside out. "I'm a redneck born into a sharecropper family from the poorest of the poor counties in Georgia. I never graduated high school. Worked the land until the red dirt seemed rooted in my pores. When I got the hell away, the Marines helped me get my G.E.D., then taught me how to kill a man in so many different ways, I'm not sure I can even list them all."

And that was supposed to scare her off? Not even. She admired him for overcoming his background and becoming a success in the rarified world of special operations.

Sam walked slowly toward the bed, his steady gaze never leaving her. "And while the military might've also pounded some manners and even more education into me ... scratch the surface, sweetheart, and I'm still the country boy who poached game to feed his family. I'm not nearly good enough for the daughter of an earl."

He stopped by the side of the bed. His eyes were hooded, hiding his emotions. But she could read her Marine like a book. *Bloody buggering hell.* Sam needed her and was holding back, reining himself in ... because she was born with blue blood?

As she opened her mouth to set him straight, he spoke—

"So ... if you don't want me, don't want this"—he indicated his ferociously aroused cock pushing against his boxers—"plus all the history and baggage that comes with me, tell me now. Because, little cat—"

With less than steady fingers, Sam tenderly smoothed hair off her face and tucked it behind her ear. "Once I have you, I'm never gonna let you go."

Men ... so bleeding blind at times.

"Not want you?" Dawn rose to her knees and wrapped her arms around his neck. "What a..." She kissed his forehead. "...load of..." Trailing a hand over his shoulder, she felt the tense muscles relax as she petted him and peppered kisses over his face. "...rubbish."

"It's not rubbish, it's the truth," he growled as he pulled her nakedness flush against his tightly muscled body. "I'm not like the sophisticated men you're used to. Your family would be appalled if you took me home."

"My family will adore you." She nipped his lower lip, then licked it. "And for your information, I've searched for a real man—one exactly like you … one like my father who also turned his back on his past and became his own man—for the longest time. I don't want some wanker like Lloyd with his sense of entitlement."

Sam pulled away from her and stared into her eyes. He was reading her again.

Mere seconds later, he shook his head and muttered, "Sweet Jesus, you really mean it." Then he pulled her flush against him and took her mouth, thrusting his tongue inside, conquering her mouth, claiming every inch.

This man was an unexpected gift from the gods. One she'd never thought to receive, but that she'd gratefully accept for as long as fate allowed.

Moaning into his ravening kiss, she clutched his shoulders and rubbed her naked breasts against his chest. Her nipples pebbled to sharp points as her nipple rings snagged on his chest hair. When his stiff cock poked her abdomen, her pussy reacted, clenching on a terrible, aching emptiness.

"Off." She tugged at the waistband of his boxers.

"Bossy, little cat." Laughing, he stepped back and dropped his boxer-briefs, then stood motionless, gloriously naked and highly aroused.

"Um—" She swallowed hard.

Hell, she'd known his cock was large—after all, his underwear had outlined his cock nicely—but seeing his hard-on in all its magnificence brought home just how big and thick he really was.

"Will that even fit?" she squeaked out.

He stepped closer, moving slowly as if he were afraid she'd bolt, and then rubbed his hands up and down her arms. "Yes … eventually."

She trembled under his gentle touch.

"I know," she said. Under his patient, affectionate gaze, she took several deep breaths, then licked suddenly dry lips. "I want this"—she ran a finger along the length of his stiff shaft, the blue veins standing out in stark relief—"in me, but—"

"But only after you're ready for me." He lowered her to lie on her back on the bed. "That's my job. Multiple orgasms should help."

She swallowed hard. Multiple orgasms? She'd never had more than one orgasm in any of her sexual encounters. She'd thought they were an urban legend.

"My body's ready." She looked up and found he wore a loving, but slightly amused expression. "I've been aching and wet since you ripped my bathing suit off. It's my brain that's sending out warning signals about mathematical impossibilities."

"Funny girl. We'll fit." He covered her body with his, keeping his weight off her by propping himself on his forearms.

She sighed at the heat radiating off him. He was like a living, breathing blanket. Wonderful.

"That swimsuit was sinful temptation." His voice was low and rumbly like the harsh purr of a jungle cat. "The kind of wicked seduction the Lord would smite a poor, ole Georgia boy for."

Dawn laughed. "Did the Lord smite you a lot while you were growing up?"

"Nope, but my daddy did." He grinned, a sexy little twist of his lips. "I had lots of ungodly thoughts, little cat. Still do."

"About me?" She smoothed her hands over his shoulders and down his arms, delighting at the supple, tanned skin stretched over prominent muscles.

"Hell, yeah." Bracing on one arm, he cradled one of her breasts in his hand, squeezing it gently. "From the first moment you called me crock-of-shit. Call me perverse, but I like a feisty woman." Then he tugged lightly on one of her nipple rings.

The sharp twinge of pain he caused morphed into a frisson of pleasure that shot straight to her core. She moaned and arched into his touch. "Sam-m-m—"

"Jesus, you have perfect breasts." He lowered his head and licked around the edge of the areola, avoiding the tip. "So sweet." Then he sucked the hardened tip into his mouth, tangling his tongue in the ring.

"Oh, God, please … more." Dawn reached for his head. Threading her fingers in his thick hair, she held him to her breast as he suckled her nipples and teethed the rings, sending ripples of pleasure over her body. "So bloody good."

She thrust her body upward and rubbed herself against his hot shaft. His precum trailed over her bare mound. His cock jerked and even more precum moistened her skin.

Sam was holding back. His body was rigid, held tensely above her; his expression was a rictus of pain. He probably thought she wasn't ready. Hell, if she were any more ready, she'd be coming. She'd gotten wet, aching, and needy merely from the thought of taking him inside her body. Truth be told, she'd been at a low boil since Cartagena.

"Take me. Play later. I need you." She clamped her legs around his lean hips in an attempt to maneuver him closer to her opening. "Now."

Sam released her nipple and moved to nuzzle and lick the valley between her breasts. "Such a greedy, little cat."

"Bloody right." She licked a path up his throat to his ear and then bit the lobe. "I'm so-o-o close, luv. I haven't had a cock in me for well over a year. Think how good my pussy will feel. I'll be so tight…"

Dawn squealed as Sam surged upward and back into a kneeling position. He pulled her body upright, her hips aligned with his, and then positioned her legs, one over each of his thighs. His cock throbbed against her pussy lips. It would take only a slight adjustment and he'd be in her.

"Don't move away," he gritted out.

"I won't." She gripped his waist with both hands. "Hurry."

Sam grabbed a condom from a pile on the bed.

When had he put those there? She grinned. Marines must always be prepared, sort of like Boy Scouts.

Sam ripped one packet open with his teeth and rolled the condom onto his penis in what had to be a land speed record. That was so not a Boy Scout move.

"Hold onto my shoulders," he muttered through clenched teeth. His voice sounded pained.

She stroked and petted her way from his waist to his chest—where she massaged his nipples.

"Don't tease me, sweetheart. I'm riding the edge here."

She shot him a naughty grin and tweaked one of his nipples before stroking her way to his shoulders—slowly. Very slowly. "I'm not teasing, luv. I am very seriously seducing you."

"Dawn," he uttered in a warning tone. "I need to go slow. Don't want to hurt you."

"You won't." She held onto his shoulders and stared into his hot, fierce gaze. "Take me, Marine."

"Fuck, yeah." Placing a hand on each side of her hips, Sam pulled her toward his large, thick—*God, so thick*—cock.

She swallowed and watched through heavily lidded eyes as he nudged the large head into her wet, swollen opening.

"Eyes. On me." His voice was rough, gravelly, like a country lane.

Dawn dragged her gaze from the dark plum-red head of his cock to look at his face. His expression was strained with ferocious concentration—and worry and love.

Could this man get any better? The visual evidence proved he could. He was so concerned he'd hurt her, not give her pleasure, that he was putting himself through hell. Didn't he understand that merely being with him did it for her?

Obviously not.

"Sam ... luv—" She brushed a kiss over his thinned lips. "I'm been aching for you." She inhaled. "Your scent. Being near you. Trading insults with you. All of it's been foreplay. Better than any I've ever had before. Just kissing you is better than any intercourse I've ever had. I need you … because this"—she moved forward until his cock head was inside her and then moaned—"us … is so fucking right."

Holding even more tightly onto his shoulders, she shoved herself fully onto his cock.

"Bloody hell." She threw her head back and let out a low, throaty groan. "So fucking full." She dropped her forehead onto his shoulder and panted as her channel stretched and strained to accommodate his length and breadth. "God, I feel your heartbeat in my pussy."

"What the fuck, sweetheart? Are you nuts?" He rubbed his cheek gently over her hair. "I'm gonna pull out. Kiss and pet your pussy…"

"Don't you fucking dare." She pressed her hips more tightly against his. "Move that fine arse, Marine. I'm so fucking close…" She turned and lightly bit his shoulder.

"Fuck, little hellcat."

"Just move." She squeezed his cock with her inner muscles and a light spasm had her keening. "So good." She kissed her way from his shoulder to his chest and took one of his nipples in her mouth and teethed it.

He shouted, "Fuck!" The shocked look on his face made her giggle and she clamped down on his cock once more.

"Sweetheart, you're killing me," he muttered.

Then it was her turn to groan as he withdrew his cock several inches and then drove it back into her, setting up a fast, hard rhythm. Each powerful thrust hit a ultra-sensitive spot inside her, shooting shards of heated pleasure throughout the deepest part of her body. Each withdrawal made her mewl as his thick cock lit fires along her most sensitive tissue. With each thrust-pull, pressure built until she thought she'd go mad as she strained to find the ultimate pleasure.

"Sam," she sank her nails into his shoulders, "I need … more."

And he gave it to her. Holding her to him with one hand on her hip, he slowed his hip movement and inserted his other hand between their bodies and fingered her clit. A blast of the most intense pleasure-pain swept over her like a firestorm, cutting her loose from the confines of her body and sending her mind-spirit soaring. Her senses floated on heated waves of pleasure as her body shuddered and trembled with the strength of her orgasm.

Dawn came and came and came. She moaned, gasped, and muttered only God knew what. All awareness of time and space was lost in the overwhelming sensations sweeping over and through her body.

The one thing anchoring her to the earth was Sam. Her Marine held her through the conflagration, whispering words of love and praise—and grinding his cock into her, milking her climax until she collapsed, utterly spent, against him.

"Told you," she mumbled against his lightly furred chest. "I was ready." She rubbed her cheek over his sweaty skin. Then she lifted her head and found his gaze on her. He was smiling, a gentle loving expression. One she definitely wanted to see every day for the rest of her life.

"Yeah, you did." He kissed the tip of her nose. His cock was still lodged deeply inside her, throbbing like the base notes in a heavy metal song. "Hold on, sweetheart, because you're going to come again, and this time I plan on joining you."

"Um, luv, I'm not—" She wasn't sure she could climax again. But she didn't care. She liked the feel of him pulsating inside her, even though his cock stretched her to the point of painful pleasure. It felt like bleeding heaven and hell at the same time.

"Oh, you will. Trust me." He held her arse steady for his rhythmic, steady thrusts and used the fingers of his free hand to rub circles over and around her clitoral hood. Every so often he thumbed her oh-so-sensitive clit, still engorged with blood from the last build-up.

Her breath hitched as he rebuilt the tension inside her core.

"I want you to crave this," he murmured against her cheek. "Crave me."

"I already do. Sam-m-m, you need to move harder … again." Shocked at how quickly her need had reawakened, she clutched his shoulders, digging in with her nails. "I ache again."

"Good." He expelled a harsh breath. "I'm gonna take care of it." His face was red and sweaty from the control he exerted while building her need once again.

"Yes-s-s-s … good … so bloody good." A syncopated pulsing began inside her pussy. His cock throbbed in counterpoint to her sheath squeezing him. She arched into his body, taking his cock so deeply it bumped her cervix. "Ahh." She winced at the flash of pain which quickly dissipated.

A slap to the outside of her hip startled her. But even that sharp bite of pain also added to the pleasure climbing toward an explosive peak.

"What?" She blinked at him.

"You hurt yourself." He settled both hands on her hips. "I'm holding the reins here." A muscle in his jaw pulsed and his arms bulged. "Later, I'll take you as roughly and deeply as you want. Right now—" He threw his head back and closed his eyes as she clamped down on his cock, but still he managed to hold onto his control. "I'm makin' love to my woman … my small, tight, sex-starved woman."

Dawn laughed, then sobbed her pleasure as Sam began a steady thrusting of his hips. "God, luv. Faster." She slapped at his shoulder.

"Fuck, yeah." Sam lowered her onto the bed until she was flat on her back. Then he braced himself over her and pounded into her until her breasts bounced wildly and the bed thumped against the wall.

With each downstroke, he ground his pubic bone over her clit, causing her to gasp at the piercing ecstasy. When he pulled out, she mewled at the loss. Gasp. Mewl. Gasp. Mewl. The cycle repeated at an ever increasing speed until once again fevered bliss and Sam were her only realities.

"God, you feel so fucking good." Sam placed biting kisses along her jaw and then sucked her ear lobe between his lips. When she moved a hand to rub then pinch his nipple in return, he muttered, "Little hellcat," and he teethed the lobe he suckled.

Her breath hitched and she arched her neck, giving him full access to her throat and very sensitive ears.

"Is that a hot spot, little cat?" He licked along the rim of her ear and then lightly bit the lobe.

"Yes-s-s," she hissed as he nipped his way to the other ear.

"Good." He lovingly tormented her other lobe, then kissed and sucked his way to a nipple where he teethed the ring.

The tug on her nipples was like a shot of electricity straight to her core. She cried out and arched into his touch.

"Love these." He took her nipple into his mouth and tongued the ring. Her pussy spasmed with each flick of his agile tongue. "I'm gonna buy you diamonds for these tasty little buds."

"Sam ... so ... so close." She arched her body into each of his thrusts now. "I ... need..."

"This." Sam pummeled her hips just as he lifted one hand to thumb then tug on the nipple ring.

Dawn couldn't breathe. The bite of pain exacerbated the pressure escalating inside her. Her world view had narrowed to pure sensation. The feel of his cock dragging along overly sensitized nerves inside her pussy. The piercing pleasure-pain concentrated in the little bundle of nerves at the apex of her thighs. The brush of rough chest hair over her tender nipples. The scent of their combined musks as their heated bodies threw off pheromones. The feel of sweat on her skin as she strove to reach her peak and then dive into free fall. The sound of Sam's grunts and groans and his muttered "so sweet, so fucking sweet" harmonizing with her gasps and cries as they sought the ultimate pleasure—together.

Then in one perfect moment, the mundane sensory world disappeared, blasted out of her consciousness, and was replaced with a tsunami of pure pleasure. She thought she screamed his name, but after that, all words … language … failed her. All she could do was moan, mewl, and sigh as her body was taken over by a force more powerful than her will.

As she was tossed about on a sea of pleasure, Sam roared her name and joined her in free fall. Their orgasms fed upon one another, dipping and swirling, for what seemed like an eternity.

Floating down from one of the highest highs she'd ever experienced, she heard Sam crooning against her neck. "Love this. So precious. My little cat. So perfect."

Her arms feeling strangely boneless, she stroked his back as they lay face-to-face. They were still connected, his cock, amazingly, still hard inside her. He anchored her to him, his arms around her body, as if he never wanted to let go, never wanted to be separated again.

"Can we stay like this forever?" She kissed his sweaty chest and then snuggled her face against his shoulder. She inhaled his scent and moaned. "Yummy. So addictive."

Sam laughed. The sensation rumbled over her body, touching her everywhere, inside and out.

"Sweetheart, I'm glad you find me addictive, and I'm willing to stay just like this." He nuzzled some hair off her forehead and followed the move with a gentle kiss. "But I don't think Maddox could send us out on jobs this way."

The image of chasing bad guys while nude and connected at the hip had Dawn giggling so hard, she snorted into his chest. Sam held her through her fit of giggles, petting her back and arse in long, slow strokes.

When she finally caught her breath, she found him smiling at her. "I don't think I've ever laughed in bed before. I like it. I like you, too, Sam Crocker. My MacCrocker and sometimes my Crock-of-shit."

Sam held her chin and brushed kisses over her face. Pausing, he whispered against her forehead, "That's when I knew I had to have you."

"When was that, luv?" She turned her face into his palm and kissed it.

"In Belize, when you hissed at me like the cutest little cat and called me names." He took her mouth in a gentle, but no less hungry kiss.

Dawn returned the kiss, which grew deeper and more ravenous until they both moaned and pulled away.

"Jesus, sweetheart," Sam said. "You go to my head like good shine."

"Shine?" She scrunched her nose.

"Moonshine." He kissed the tip of her nose. "Homemade grain alcohol, guaranteed to knock you on your sweet ass."

"Hmmm—" She massaged his shoulders and then smoothed her hands up and down his strongly muscled arms. His cock was hard and throbbing inside her again. His recovery time was impressive.

Her internal clock told her the real world would intrude soon, but first—"Let me take care of this hard problem you seem to have." She clamped her vaginal muscles around his thick shaft.

Sam raised his head. His silver grey eyes had darkened to pewter. "Sweetheart, you're gonna be sore."

Dawn patted his cheek. "I'll live. I want you, Sam. I want to sit at that card table tonight and still feel you inside me."

"Little cat," he breathed out and then took her lips with a deep, ravenous kiss before breaking off. "My hellcat."

Her Marine, his gaze fixed on her face, pulled her top leg up and over his hips, then began the rhythmic hip movement that could only end in their mutual pleasure once more. As Dawn fell under the sway of his lovemaking, she let go of all thoughts of perverted sheiks, dead poisonous snakes, traitors, and what tonight might bring and replaced them with fantasies of a future when Sam said the words that matched his actions.

When he gave her the words, she'd tell him she loved him, too.

CHAPTER 10

March 3rd, 7:45 p.m.

Dawn checked her image in the full-length mirror on the back of the bathroom door. "Bloody hell, I look like a bleeding prostitute."

The dress was tight, tighter than anything she'd ever worn. So tight, she couldn't wear a bra or even knickers. The color was blush pink, a color so light she looked as if she wasn't wearing anything at all.

It was too late now to find something else to wear. Later, she'd definitely have a few choice words for Keely about this little outfit. The dress belonged to Keely. Something told Dawn that Ren had ordered his wife to get rid of the dress.

Hindsight said Dawn should've tried it on before she left Cartagena.

Balancing precariously on four-inch heels, she made her way out of the bathroom. A longing glance at the rumpled bed brought back memories of all the lovely, delicious things Sam had done to her body hours earlier—and while he hadn't actually told her he loved her, he'd shown her with every touch, every glance.

Dawn sighed. She hadn't liked waking up from her much-needed nap to an alarm—and alone with only a note for company. The note said *"You needed your rest. If I'd stayed that wouldn't have happened. I'll be watching over you this evening. Stay safe, little cat. – Sam."*

Her first sort of love note from a man. A very special man. She'd tucked the missive in her passport for safe-keeping.

Time to go to work. Tapping at her diamond-studded smart watch, she activated her com system and the camera in her necklace. "Systems check."

"Hey, Dawn." Ren's voice.

Her mood sank. Where was Sam?

"I hear you loud and clear," Ren said. "Camera shows a nice image of the door of your suite. We'll adjust the angle of the camera feed once you're seated at the Baccarat table."

"Roger that. You're also coming across loud and clear. Is Conn in place?" she asked.

"Conn's at the table, sweetheart." Sam's deep voice and the loving way he said "sweetheart" sent a flush of recalled pleasure over her body. "I've told him his job is to protect your sweet ass. Let him."

"I can take care of myself, luv." Her response was a knee-jerk one, a sop to her hard-worn position in a man's world. But, in reality, she understood why Sam said what he had—he cared. So she'd cut her man some slack. They were still new, feeling their way into a relationship. Eventually, he'd learn she wasn't foolhardy or wild and that she only took on risks she could handle. "Is Keely monitoring our communications?"

"Not on this frequency, but we can pull her in, if needed," Ren answered. "She's monitoring intelligence chatter, real-time satellite images, and the eyes and ears we have on MacLean's estate. She's also backing up resort security on running facial recognition on the day's video feed from the resort security cameras, trying to find Lloyd."

Ron, the fucking wanker—she couldn't even get rid of him even after she'd quit. "Hope Keely finds the arsehole."

"She will. Now, get down to the casino," Ren said, his tone almost pleading. "Conn's losing his shirt at Baccarat. Don't you lose yours."

Dawn snorted. "Wouldn't make much difference with what I'm wearing. Tell your wife I get to vet all my undercover costume choices in the future *before* I leave for an assignment."

"Shit"—Ren spoke over Sam's shouted "What the fuck?"—"which dress of hers did she lend you?"

"You'll see in a second." Dawn opened her suite door, entered the hall, and closed the door behind her, making sure it locked. Then she slowly turned toward the security camera nearest her room and blew them a kiss.

"Fuck," Ren snarled. "Ass in the fucking chair, Sam. It's too fucking late now. She has to get the fuck downstairs. Fucking Benrabi is due to show up with the fucker MacLean in tow. Dawn needs to fucking be there or we lose this opportunity."

Entering the elevator, Dawn snickered. Since she was alone, it was safe to comment. "That was a bleeding bunch of fucks, mate."

"That's because I clearly remember telling my lovely wife to burn that dress," Ren responded.

"Um, this is an Herve Leger, Ren."

"That's exactly what she told me and my reply was—"

"Fuck Leger?" Dawn filled in the blank.

"Yeah." Ren's chuckle was half-laugh, half-snarl.

"Guess she thought giving it to me was a better choice than throwing it away." Dawn blew out a breath. "Well, it will definitely draw Benrabi and his friend MacLean's attention. But I am not leaving the casino without Conn at my side, covering my scantily clad arse."

"Damn straight. If not Conn, we'll get one of Theo's security people to shadow you," Sam added, his tone as stern and sober as a judge.

"Yes, Sam." Normally, Dawn would resent the waves of testosterone-induced over-protectiveness coming from him and Ren, but in this instance, she agreed with their concern. This dress had been designed to make men's blood boil … to cause riots. There were too many hot-blooded Latinos at this resort—she must've rejected half of them at the pool this morning— and she really didn't want to defend her virtue if she didn't have to.

The elevator dinged for the casino floor. Dawn inhaled and let out a breath. "Here goes nothing. Wish me luck."

"Luck, little cat. We'll be following you on the monitors from the elevator to the table. There are no blind spots in the casino." Sam's voice was calm and all business now that this part of the op was in progress.

"Just an update," Ren said. "Besides the Aruban law officer acting as a waitress, Theo put one of his security people at your table as croupier."

Dawn hummed an "uh-huh."

Men were such worriers. She'd had fewer safeguards in place when she'd walked the docks of Marseilles as a hooker in an attempt to attract the attention of the drug-trafficking cartel leader. Shit had happened. She'd handled it.

Her current outfit was a glorified success if the responses of the men she'd passed were any indication. She smiled at a security guard who inclined his head as she walked by him and then casually began to follow her.

"Conn has arranged it so you'll sit and immediately be offered the Bank. Your Bank will have half a million dollars, USD. That should allow you to play for as long as it takes us to get MacLean's DNA," Ren offered. "Hopefully, it won't take long."

Dawn mentally snorted. She was a damn good card player and wouldn't lose Ren's—or whomever's—money. As she approached the elevated section where the Baccarat table was located, she swept the area for trouble, and found nothing that made her neck itch. She then mounted four steps.

Theo was acting as the floor man for the area. He opened the golden rope closing off the table from the common people who'd never think about dropping $10,000 on a single bet, let alone play several hands at that high-dollar amount.

"Welcome, Lady Wilson." Theo inclined his head. His appreciative gaze took her in from top to bottom and back again. "You look very lovely this evening. Quite fetching."

"Thank you." She slipped him a twenty and spoke loudly enough so everyone at the table would notice. "I'd like a Glenlivet, 16-Year, Nadurra Reserve, on the rocks, with a twist of lemon, and two bottles of unopened spring water. Put them on my tab, please. Advise the waitress that I won't require any other drinks this evening."

"I'll see to your drinks personally, milady," Theo said.

"That would be lovely. Thank you." She looked toward the table where play had paused momentarily as the decks were reshuffled and the shoe reloaded. "I think my timing was perfect to join a new game."

She approached the Baccarat table. The men present stood. "Thank you, gentlemen. Please be seated. May I sit here?" She addressed Conn.

Since he'd held the Bank last, she'd be the next in line to hold the Bank. She felt lucky and was looking forward to playing. She hoped Benrabi was late. She hadn't gambled since the last time she was home for a holiday. All of her immediate family members were avid Baccarat and poker players. The games were cutthroat; she and her father were the best players, because they were willing to take the most risks. It hadn't surprised anybody in the family when she—and not her brothers—had chosen to follow her father into the world of law enforcement.

"Please do. I'm Conner." He pulled out the chair for her.

"Thank you, Conner." Dawn smiled at him. "Please call me Dawn."

Conn sat and proceeded to introduce the rest of the players. Three seats remained empty and she realized Theo would keep anyone but Benrabi and MacLean out.

Dawn nodded politely at the other men.

"Adjust the angle of your camera, Dawn," Ren ordered. "Maybe another fifteen degrees upward."

Dawn looked at her watch as if she were receiving a text on her smart phone and made the adjustment.

"That's good, Dawn," Sam said.

The female croupier turned to Dawn. "Would madam wish to hold the Bank?"

"Madam would. What are the betting limits?" Dawn asked.

"Minimum bet is $10,000. There is no maximum. What is the value of your Bank?" the croupier asked.

"A half-million U.S. dollars."

The croupier nodded and called for the floor man. "Verifying a half-million U.S., please."

Theo approached and tapped on a small computer tablet. "Half-million is approved for Lady Wilson. Good luck to everyone."

Dawn smiled at her fellow players. "Well, I'm sure you lovely gentleman will attempt to make a nice run at my funds, but"—she eyed each man in turn, ending with Conn who looked amused—"I must warn you I'm feeling very lucky this evening."

Henri, a portly man of middle age, toasted her with his martini. "*Bonne chance*, Lady Wilson." His French accent was heavy. He'd told her he was in pharmaceuticals.

Dawn picked up the Scotch Theo had placed at her spot and returned the toast. "Good luck—and do call me Dawn. Lady Wilson sounds so stuffy."

The other men smiled and raised their drinks to her also.

Just as Conn shifted the shoe toward her, a rustling of robes preceded Sam's muttering in her ear, "Heads up. Showtime."

CHAPTER 11

The casino's security center was a dimly lit circular room. A crew of techs sat at computer stations that controlled the dozens of monitors on the walls. Each monitor focused on a different area of the casino floor and often flashed four or more images of an area at one time.

Standing in front of the monitor dedicated to the High-Roller's Baccarat table, Sam's gut clenched as he watched Benrabi smile—well, leer was more like it—at Dawn. Slime-ball bastard. He shot a quick, sharp look at Ren. "Convince me again why we had to expose Dawn in order to get DNA from MacLean."

"Because, we couldn't count on MacLean leaving his estate to gamble and drink in public." Ren heaved a sigh. "But to please a client like Benrabi he might do both. And if he doesn't relax his guard enough to drink while gambling, Dawn's in place to get his DNA by accidentally cutting him with that very special ring she's wearing. I thought we'd settled this back in Cartagena?"

"Yeah—I didn't like it then and still don't." Sam focused on the screens showing the gaming table and its occupants from the cameras worn by the croupier, Conn, and Dawn and the ones in the ceiling. If a single person made one wrong move—he'd see it.

At least Dawn wasn't seated near Benrabi, who eyed her as if she were a tasty hors d'oeuvre. The additional intel provided by SSI on the Yemeni's sexual proclivities made Sam's skin crawl. "If it were Keely sitting there—"

"She wouldn't be." Ren exhaled harshly. "I get where you're coming from, Sam. You care about Dawn. Is this going to be an issue every time I send her out on an op?"

"Yes … no…" Now it was Sam who let out a raspy breath. "Ahh, fuck it. She'd kick my ass if I stopped her from doing her job. I know she's competent, but…"

"Yeah, but—" Ren laughed. "Listen to us, are we whipped or what?"

"Not whipped"—Sam leaned closer to the monitor he was watching and peered at an area of the casino adjacent to the Baccarat table—"just in love with strong, independent women who think they're Amazons. God, I love that woman."

"Have you told her?" Ren asked.

"Not yet … we've only known each other for less a week."

"Hell, it happened on sight between me and Keely. Enjoy the ride." Ren moved to look at the screen Sam stared at so intensely. "What are you seeing that I'm not?"

Sam tapped the monitor showing an area adjacent to the elevated Baccarat area. "Could that be Lloyd? In the robes?" His finger stopped on a tall man, encased in the voluminous robes of an Arab. "His face is in the shadows of his headdress, but the angle of his head has him focusing too intently on the Baccarat table."

"Maybe he's one of Benrabi's bodyguards?" Ren turned to one of Theo's security room techs. "Can you increase the magnification on camera thirty-four in sector K?"

The tech nodded and typed in a command. The image of the suspicious man magnified ten times.

"Look at his fucking hands," Sam said. "Light-skinned. And if that's not a signet ring with a British lion crest, I'm a Yankee."

"Fuck. Odds are it's Lloyd." Ren circled the man's face with his finger and traced a line to the Baccarat players. "He's looking at Dawn, not Benrabi or even MacLean."

"We've got to get him out of there before he blows Dawn's cover." Sam stood and then sat back down. "Shit, I can't go down there. Both Lloyd and MacLean know who I am."

Ren looked grim. "When we realized Lloyd was at the resort, Keely contacted Interpol. Lloyd was canned right after Dawn left Belize. Story is Dawn's report on the Belize operation got him fired. He must've found out Dawn was here and followed her."

"Conn ... Lloyd's wearing Arabic robes and is by the roulette table on the casino floor, to your right." Sam's voice was rough from tension. "Get his ass out of there before he blows this whole op or hurts Dawn."

Conn tapped his finger on the playing surface in front of him, acknowledging he'd heard. Then he traced a circle, signaling that he'd follow through.

A consummate professional, Dawn didn't even blink at the news, nor did she turn to look at the roulette table as she calmly dealt hers and the next player's hand.

"I need to sit out the next few deals." Conn slurred his words a bit, then smiled goofily at the other players as he stood and wavered in place. "Guard my seat and winnings, Dawn?"

"Of course, Conner." Dawn inclined her head. "Take your time. Eat something or grab a coffee. I'll just fleece these lovely men of all their money and get yours when you return."

Conn laughed, picked up his drink which was apple cider and not the whiskey everyone had heard him order, and lurched away from the table as if he weren't quite steady on his feet.

Theo approached Conn and placed a hand on his shoulder. "Do you need assistance, sir?"

"No, thanks." Conn waved him off and stumbled down the steps.

"Theo, you're on Dawn until Conn gets back," Ren said.

Theo tapped his ear bud in acknowledgment, then spoke into his jaw microphone in a monotone. "Security Team B to the roulette table in Sector K for backup."

Conn moved toward the aisle behind the roulette table and as he passed the man they were sure was Lloyd, he stumbled, dumped his drink all over his target, and then fell onto him, taking them both to the floor.

Theo's men moved in quickly and helped both men up and hurried them out of the casino.

The play at the Baccarat table paused. Henri joked about Conner not holding his liquor well. Dawn chided him—and play resumed.

Sam let out the breath he held and looked at Ren. "That was close."

"Ren…" Conn's voice was calm. "It's definitely Lloyd. Theo's men are bringing him up to you. I'll waste a few minutes, pick up a large coffee, maybe order some food, and head back to the table."

"Roger that." Ren turned to Sam. "You stay on the monitors. I'll handle the peckerheaded British douchebag."

"Yeah. Probably a good idea." Sam unfisted his hands. "I really want to hit somebody right about now."

Ren laughed. "It still might happen. Keep an eye on our girl."

"My girl."

Ren shook his head and grinned. "Yeah, I was like that about Keely within seconds of meeting her … still am." He clapped Sam on the shoulder and moved to greet Theo's men who escorted the now de-robed Lloyd into the security center. The former Interpol agent wore a furious expression and pulled away from the men holding his arms.

Lloyd froze when he saw Sam and tried to back away as Ren approached.

Sam smiled. Yeah, if he were a cowardly pussy like Lloyd, he'd also want to back away from the promise of pain on Ren's face.

Turning back to the monitors, he noted Dawn's body posture was stiffer than it had been a few moments ago. Benrabi was talking at her as the croupier pulled in the losing bets placed by the last player and the punters and shoved them toward Dawn. Whatever the fucker was saying upset her, although no one else looking at her would know that. Her face was a pleasant blank, a social mask.

Sam turned up the volume on the directional microphone in the ceiling camera aimed at the table. Dawn's mike was too far from Benrabi to pick up his words clearly.

"Lady Wilson…" Benrabi's words were purred in a tone Sam was sure the Yemeni thought was sexy, but only sounded menacing. "Surely you recall the time you spent in my lovely country. Your esteemed father was posted there for two years."

"I remember it was hot and dusty and that my father and mother never let me off the embassy grounds much." Dawn's tone was stiffly polite, dismissive. "It was rather boring, if you must know."

A flash of fury swept over Benrabi's face. He wasn't as good at keeping his social mask in place as Dawn.

Sam also watched MacLean's expression as Benrabi attempted to engage Dawn. Old Syd looked very much the wealthy Brazilian in his tropical weight tux and his darkly tanned skin. His eyes were dark now; contact lenses were an easy change. But his facial bone structure had changed a lot, and if Sam hadn't been sure the fucker was Syd MacLean, his gaze would've passed over the man on the street.

Then MacLean lifted his drink to his lips and took a healthy swallow.

"He's drinking. We've got him. Play a few more hands, sweetheart." Yeah, he was ordering her again, but he didn't care. He wanted her safely away from Benrabi, who even now devoured her with his slimy gaze. "Then get your sweet ass out of there. Conn's on his way back now."

Sam glanced at Ren, who gave him a thumbs up and then turned back to face the angry Lloyd. The Brit ignored Ren and glared at Sam and then at the monitors. He could've politely pointed out to the ex-Interpol agent that ignoring Ren Maddox wasn't a smart idea, but Sam wasn't feeling generous. Lloyd had endangered Dawn and Conn, jeopardized a joint U.S.-Dutch intelligence operation. The fucker could go to jail for that.

"Back," Conn said as he sat carefully in his seat as if the world were spinning. The waitress set a cup of coffee at Conn's place and a plate with finger sandwiches on it. "Thank you, my dear," he said. The waitress inclined her head and began tidying up the table, working her way toward MacLean.

"Are you okay?" Dawn turned away from her stilted conversation with Benrabi and looked at Conn.

"Just fine." Conn arranged his chips into even stacks. "Ready to take your money, milady."

"Will never happen." Dawn looked at the next player who turned out to be MacLean. "Ready, sir?"

MacLean nodded and then swallowed the rest of his drink and shoved the glass to the side. The waitress collected the empty glass and the cocktail napkin he'd blotted his mouth on; she was careful to pick up the items so as not to contaminate his DNA. She took drink orders and hurried away.

Sam smiled. Yeah, they had the bastard.

"Your bet, Lady Wilson?" the croupier asked.

Dawn looked at her chips. "I'll bet it all."

"Senor Lazaro, do you wish to go bank?" the croupier asked MacLean.

"How much is the Bank worth at the moment?" MacLean responded.

The croupier assessed Dawn's chips. "One million U.S. dollars."

MacLean looked at his tally sheet on which a player kept track of the wins and losses. He smiled and leaned back in his chair. "I'll go bank."

The rest of the players, now effectively blocked from betting, buzzed with excitement.

At Dawn's bet, Ren had come over and looked over Sam's shoulder. "Is she fucking nuts?"

"She's always like that," Lloyd said from behind them. Theo's men stood on each side of him, boxing him in. "Bloody crazy cunt."

Sam growled. "Can I kill him, Ren? I don't work for you—"

"Yet," Ren said.

"—so it won't reflect on SSI at all. The CIA can bury him deep," Sam finished.

"You blokes are barmy," sputtered Lloyd, his expression a mixture of anger and incredulity.

"And you tried to kill Dawn." Sam turned and glared at Lloyd, who didn't have the sense to know he should be worried about his immediate future. "You're fucking lucky to be fucking breathing."

"I wasn't trying to kill her," Lloyd yelled. "Just scare her. She hates snakes."

Sam surged to his feet and advanced upon Lloyd. The security men stepped away as Sam punched the man who'd threatened his woman.

Lloyd stayed on the ground and rubbed his jaw. "Are you bleeding nuts? It was just a little snake. She'd have screamed and had a right good scare, that's all."

Sam stood over him and yelled, "It was poisonous, you fucker. She could've been killed. You're fucking lucky we figured out something was wrong."

The look of surprise on the asshole's face proved the moronic peckerhead hadn't known the snake was dangerous. Then Lloyd paled as he probably realized he was lucky not to have been bitten, either.

"Jesus H. Christ, what a dumb ass. Pick him up and get him out of here," Ren instructed Theo's men. "The intelligence officer from the Dutch marine base will hold him until the local authorities decide whether they want to charge him locally with attempted murder or turn him over to the United States for attempted murder of an intelligence contractor and interference with a mission of national security."

"National security?" Lloyd blustered as he tried to shrug off the guards' hands. "What bloody national security? I thought this was all about catching Oraio and he's a bloody drug trafficker."

"Nope, this is about Oraio being Syd MacLean, U.S. traitor and trafficker of arms, drugs, humans, and intelligence secrets," Ren said.

"Oh, bloody hell. I'm fucked." Lloyd turned a sickly green and would've collapsed if the men hadn't been holding him by the elbows.

"Yeah, and be glad you are," Sam added. "Or you'd have to deal with me. Now, shut the fuck up. Dawn's dealing."

The drama unfolding in the casino now held everyone in the security center in thrall as they focused on the high stakes card game. It was like a train wreck—no one could look away.

"Deal, please, Lady Wilson," the croupier directed.

Dawn dealt one card to herself, then one to MacLean, both face down. Then dealt another to her and to MacLean, also face down. They looked at their cards.

Dawn flipped hers over. "Natural nine."

The men at the table and everyone who watched the play from the sidelines seemed to inhale at the same time. It was as if they'd all been frozen in place.

"Senor Lazaro, do you wish another card?" the croupier asked. If he had a natural nine he would've turned it over by now.

Grim-faced, he nodded. Dawn dealt another card face down. MacLean looked at it and his face grew dark. He turned his cards up. He had a total of six.

The men at the table and the people watching cheered and shouted.

"The Bank wins," the croupier intoned.

Sam laughed. "Fuck me. My ballsy little cat did it. She beat the bastard."

Ren blew out a breath and muttered, "Thank fuck. I didn't know how I was going to explain a gambling loss to the DIA."

"Fuck. The bleeding bitch has all the luck. Always has." Lloyd sounded like a whiny teenager, blaming everyone but himself for the mess he was in. "And when she doesn't rely on luck, she uses her father's position to screw people over. She got me fired."

Sam turned toward the security guards. "Why isn't he gone yet?"

The men saluted and dragged Lloyd away.

"Dawn, play another hand or two to pacify the rest of the table and then surrender the Bank," Ren ordered.

Dawn tapped the table once in acknowledgment.

Sam looked at Ren. "Do we know yet if we got enough of a sample on MacLean?"

Ren checked his smart phone. "The forensic tech the DIA sent down said there was enough saliva on the glass to do the DNA test. The waitress who's a tech for the Aruban police was smart to bag the napkin since they also managed to get skin cells and sweat. So we can run three tests—and if they match MacLean's DNA on file, the Dutch will extradite him immediately to the United States."

"Now, all we have to do is catch him and Benrabi in the act of slave trafficking, so we can hold MacLean long enough to get the DNA results back," Sam said.

A push notification sounded loudly in the room and Ren checked his phone once again then grinned. "Good news. We can take immediate custody of MacLean. My creative wife recorded MacLean's voice during the card game and then hit up some of her NSA buddies and obtained some recordings of

MacLean when he was at the DIA. She just finished running a match against the audio from the card game. It's an exact match."

"Hoo-rah," Sam said.

Ren tapped a message on his phone and hit send. "I just gave the Dutch military the go-ahead to take control of Benrabi and MacLean's yachts and the container ship as part of our pursuit of a U.S. traitor and his associates. They'll also take over MacLean's estate," Ren said. "Discovery of the kidnapped girls on the ship can only add nails to both asshats' coffins."

"When do we take MacLean and Benrabi into custody?" Sam's gaze never left Dawn as she dazzled her fellow players and continued to win.

"After they leave the casino," Ren said. "We don't want any innocents hurt in the takedown. Damn, Dawn's either the luckiest card player in the world or the croupier stacked the shoe somehow."

"Bet you're glad MacLean will finally be contained," said Sam.

"The fucking bastard tried to kill Keely and others in the SSI family." Ren smiled, an ugly smile. "Worst fucking mistake he ever made."

Sam was glad he and Ren were on the same side. The man was scary in his retribution, and not much scared Sam.

CHAPTER 12

Dawn smiled brightly as the croupier pulled in MacLean's bet and pushed the chips toward her position. "Well, that was lucky. What's say we see how long my winning streak will last?"

"Conn. Dawn…" Ren's deep voice came over her ear bud. "We have what we need. Wrap this up and get the fuck out of there. We'll be taking MacLean and Benrabi into custody right after they leave the hotel."

Thank God. A couple more hands was about all she could handle. Being this close to Benrabi made her skin crawl more than she'd imagined.

A bright smile on her face, she continued stacking her winnings while wondering what the fuck was going on. The original plan had been to catch MacLean and Benrabi in the act of transferring the girls from the container ship to Benrabi's yacht. Whatever had changed had not altered her or Conn's next moves.

Initiating their exit plan, Conn moved closer to her. He placed an arm along the back of her chair and played with her hair. "Have dinner with me?"

Dawn turned toward him and gave him a dazzling smile. "Yes, thank you. Let me play a few more hands?"

"Sure. Give 'em hell, babe." His wink and the smile he gave her would probably have melted the knickers off a more susceptible female.

But she was immune. Her knickers and the removal thereof were solely in the keeping of Sam.

Dawn finished stacking her chips and consulted her tally sheet. "My calculations have me winning at slightly over sixty-two percent. Odds are that won't last. Anyone feeling lucky?"

Henri, who'd flirted with her outrageously since she'd sat down, saluted her with his brandy. "Deal, milady. You have to lose now. The … how do they say it in America? … the elephant is no longer in the room."

Conn laughed. "Close enough. Deal, babe. I missed several hands." He looked at his watch. "Maybe I can recoup some of my losses before our dinner reservation at an exclusive little restaurant on the beach I discovered."

"That sure of me, Conner?" She punched him lightly on the arm. "You made the reservation even before asking me. What if I'd said no?"

"I'd have kept asking until you said yes." Conn captured her hand and kissed the tips of her fingers. "I'm very persuasive when I see something I want."

Conn was definitely laying the lover act on thick. And Benrabi was buying it if his stiff body language was any indicator. The Yemeni uttered several curses during a lengthy diatribe. While her Arabic—and the Yemeni dialect in question—were rusty, roughly translated, he'd likened Conn to camel dung, called her a filthy whore, and ended his tirade by calling down the curses of Allah on the Earl of Oxenham for his perfidy in keeping her from the sheikh.

MacLean smirked at his partner-in-crime's harangue, but jerked when her father's title was mentioned. He turned a piercing look on Dawn. For several seconds, his expression was almost analytical as if he were examining and rejecting hypotheses. Then his lips quirked in a crooked half smile that gave her a really bad feeling in the pit of her stomach.

Her only conclusion? The arsehole knew her father and knew he was in British intelligence.

MacLean leaned over and whispered something in Benrabi's ear which caused the sheikh to nod. Then the bleeding traitor texted someone.

Now, that didn't bode well for Conn or her—or SSI's mission.

"Don't worry about them, sweetheart," Sam's voice sounded a bit strained. He'd obviously picked up on the odd MacLean-Benrabi interchange. "Just stick close to Conn. We'll have eyes on them and you at all times."

But that wouldn't tell them to whom MacLean had sent a message or what it had contained. She had a sinking feeling they'd find the answer to both those concerns sooner or later.

She tapped a finger on the table, acknowledging Sam's communication. But she wouldn't relax her guard until Benrabi and MacLean were locked away.

"Bets, please," the croupier called.

Lost in thought, Dawn startled.

Conn patted her hand as he leaned in to whisper, "You okay?"

She nodded. "Sorry, just calculating how much more I need to win to buy the little island off the coast of the Bahamas that I'm interested in."

Several of the players laughed. The Ukrainian player said, "I'll buy you an island. Ditch the American and fly away with me."

"Sorry, but I've already promised to dine with Conner." She sent the other man a smoldering gaze. "Ask me again tomorrow evening, I might have changed my mind about the Yank by then."

"I'll look for you." The Ukrainian raised his glass of vodka and saluted her.

Dawn turned to the croupier. "Let's start out easy. Give the gents a chance to catch up. Banker bets ten thousand."

The next player didn't have the funds to go bank so he matched her bet. The punters kicked in ten thousand a piece. Even MacLean—whose unnerving attention had kept returning to her since Benrabi mentioned her father—kicked in a bet.

The traitor's smile had turned decidedly cruel. But Benrabi's expression was even scarier. Something told her if the sheikh got his hands on her, she'd fare no better than the young girls he planned to pimp to his radical allies. Rape would be the least of the horrors she'd face.

Keeping her face pleasantly bland, Dawn took a deep breath and dealt the cards. She won again. And then again on the next deal.

"Time to wind this up, sweetheart." Sam's voice over the com system was more than welcome.

While most of her fellow players were exclaiming at her marvelous run of luck and that it had to end soon, MacLean and Benrabi were silent. They had about them the air of patient predators—and she was positive they weren't planning to beat her at cards.

"One more hand, gentlemen," she aimed a bright smile at Conn, "then my new American friend is taking me to dinner."

"And maybe a walk along the beach?" Conn covered her ice-cold hand with his warm one. "I'd love to see how your skin looks in the moonlight."

Dawn pulled her hand out from under Conn's and organized her new winnings into stacks. "We'll see how dinner goes first, shall we?"

Conn nodded. "Of course."

The croupier called for bets. Dawn raised her bet to twenty thousand this round, and the player, Benrabi this time, matched it. Several others dropped out, but MacLean stayed in with a matching bet. She dealt the cards. She had an eight and had to turn it over.

"Another card, Sheikh?" She arched an eyebrow.

He scowled and looked at his cards again as if they'd changed since he'd looked at them a second or so ago. "Card."

Dawn dealt him a five face up. Benrabi swore and turned over his cards, both face cards worth zero. "You win again, Lady Dawn." He stared at her as if he could see into her brain. "I would like a chance to regain some of my money. Maybe you would join me and my friend on my yacht for a private game?"

"I'd be happy to give you and"—she looked toward MacLean—"Senor Lazaro a chance to win back some of your funds ... but it would have to be here in the casino. I'm afraid I get horribly seasick."

Benrabi shrugged. "Tomorrow, then. Here. Eight o'clock?" He stood quickly while MacLean got up more slowly.

She'd bet her winnings that Benrabi planned on seeing her long before tomorrow. Little did he know, he'd be in custody when he did.

"That would be marvelous. See you then." She turned toward Conn. "Conner, do we have time to cash in my chips?"

Conn shook his head. "Our reservation is soon."

Theo came to their side. "Lady Wilson, if you wish, I will cash your chips in for you and have them put the amount on your account. Allow me to give you a receipt for them."

"Thank you. That would be lovely." She counted the chips. "My math says I have two million four hundred thousand."

"That agrees with my count." Theo handed her his tablet and she signed the screen. He printed out a receipt for her. "Enjoy the rest of your evening."

MacLean and Benrabi left the Baccarat area just as Theo moved away from her and Conn.

Conn pulled out her chair and assisted her in standing. They exchanged goodbyes with the other players.

"The targets are taking the hall toward the parking garage," Sam reported. "Get Dawn out of there, Conn, and then come round to the parking garage exit to join us."

Conn took her arm by the elbow and assisted her down the stairs, then steered her toward the main lobby of the resort.

"Guys," Dawn said. "Something else is going on with MacLean and Benrabi, something aside from completing their slave-trafficking business this evening. Benrabi calmed down far too quickly after Conn's Don Juan routine." She looked over her shoulder and didn't see anything out of the norm, but still her neck itched like crazy. "Are you sure they're on their way to their car, Sam?"

"They're in the garage now," Sam said. "When they drive out, they'll be stopped and arrested. Ren and I are on our way to assist on that take-down now."

"What changed?" Dawn asked as Conn maneuvered them through the crowds. "Why arrest them now?"

"We have positive proof that Oraio the sex trafficker is MacLean, U.S. traitor," Sam said. "Keely matched voice prints on MacLean. The local authorities are comfortable holding him for the United States on that evidence alone. Ren advised the Dutch navy to go ahead and seize the container ship and rescue the girls. The Dutch marines have seized computers and files from MacLean's estate and Benrabi's yacht tying them to the slave trading."

"So, no reason to wait," Dawn said. "That's bloody marvelous."

"Damn straight," Sam replied.

"Get the arseholes," Dawn said. "I'll just go sit with the other helpless little woman as we wait for our men to come home from the wars."

Okay, so she was a little bit pissed at not being there when bloody Benrabi was taken into custody. She'd live.

Conn laughed as he smoothly and swiftly moved her through the throng in the lobby.

"Dawn"—Ren's voice—"MacLean recognized your father's name. I'm not taking any chances with your safety. So, you'll go to the estate and keep Keely company. We've got this covered."

"Um, got the message, mate." Dawn's response was terse. Her skin prickled as if dozens of spiders crawled over her. Something wasn't right. She surveyed her surroundings, but saw nothing that indicated she and Conn were under observation. But still—her fingers clenched and unclenched and she wished her gun was more easily accessible. She was sure pulling her dress up in public to draw her gun from her thigh holster wasn't a good move at the moment. But as soon as she got outside, she'd risk the exposure and retrieve her weapon.

"Sweetheart…" An apologetic tone had entered Sam's voice. "…Old Syd would love to get a twist on someone in MI6 since he's lost all his NSA connections. He'd take you and use you as leverage in New York minute."

She huffed out an exasperated breath. "Luv, I know that. Plus, after the come-on Conn gave me and my acceptance of the same, Benrabi would torture and rape me and then turn me over to his men to do the same. Do you all think I was born yesterday?"

"Sam and I know you're not stupid or inexperienced in the field," Ren said. "And I never meant to imply that. It's just—"

"It's just that you're a controlling, dominant male and my skill sets are not needed now," Dawn finished.

"That about sums it up," Ren agreed.

She shook her head and pinched Conn's arm when he had the audacity to laugh again. As she was new to SSI and her boss had not seen in her action before, she would cut Ren some slack.

Dawn and Conn exited the hotel. Theo had beat them outside and now spoke with a man in a Dutch marine uniform, leaning against the driver's side door. An argument ensued.

"Bloody hell, my neck's never wrong." Dawn pulled Conn to a halt. "Something's wrong." She bent down, jerked her dress up—which was a battle since it fit like a second skin— and then drew her weapon. She tugged the skirt back over her arse one-handed just as Theo and the man began to fight.

She brought her gun up and aimed it at the man attacking Theo. She didn't have a clear shot and Theo definitely was getting the worse end of the fight.

"Conn, the arsehole has a knife," Dawn shouted.

Theo didn't.

"Fuck." Conn ran toward the fighting men. "Ren ... Sam, Dawn's ride was compromised. Need some backup here."

"I'm your bloody backup," Dawn snarled.

"Dawn, get the fuck out of there," Sam said. "Ren and I are on our way."

"Fuck that, luv. I'm not leaving my partner." Dawn covered Conn's ass while he attempted to help Theo. Her gaze swept the valet parking area; her gun arm tracked her visual scan.

No response from her Marine, just the sounds of his breathing and his pounding footsteps echoing in the background.

"Dawn. Conn—" Ren's calm voice came over the com. "Heads up, we lost visual on MacLean and Benrabi. They're in the wind. They could be heading your way."

"Roger that," muttered Dawn. She backed toward Conn and the two fighting men, counting on Conn to have that direction covered. She figured any new attack would come from the hotel or the parking garage set off to the side of the valet parking area. Those were the areas she now watched like a hawk.

Over her ear bud, she heard Ren issuing orders in a clipped, urgent tone and the sounds of multiple pounding feet. Help was coming, but would it arrive soon enough?

Her neck said not.

Conn shouted, "Theo, watch out," and a shot rang out.

Male groans of pain sent chills down her spine. Had Conn been shot?

She looked over her shoulder. Theo was on the ground, a knife in his chest and far too much blood already pooling on the ground. His assailant was also down—gut shot and lying in his own pool of blood.

"Ren ...Theo's hurt ... we need paramedics." Dawn ran toward Conn who after checking the downed thug for weapons and restraining him had then moved to kneel by Theo's side.

When she reached Conn and Theo, she placed her body between them and the almost palpable danger still lurking in the shadows. She felt the renewed threat clawing at her throat, making it harder for her to breathe. Her finger tightened on the trigger of her weapon, but she had no target. She couldn't get a positive direction for whatever was triggering her fight-or-flight reaction. "Come on, you bloody arses, show yourselves."

"Dawn, get the fuck inside," Conn ordered. "I got this ... shit ... shit—Ren, we need a medic now."

"I'm staying, mate." She looked over her shoulder and found Conn had taken off his sport coat and was using it to apply pressure around the chest wound. The fact Conn had left the knife in Theo's chest and the blood was already soaking the thick fabric weren't good signs.

Dawn surveilled the area. "You're the only thing keeping Theo alive. I plan on keeping you alive until help gets here."

"Dawn ... Benrabi and MacLean know their original business is fucked. It's you they'll want now. You're leverage." Ren's voice. "Get to the registration desk and stay there. Sam's coming through the casino now. He can back up Conn. I'll be there soon after."

Her gut told her to stay with Conn and Theo, but her boss had ordered her to leave. Fuck it. She went with her gut and stayed where she was, continuing a visual sweep of the area.

Movement caught her eye. Black flowing over black in the shadows of the valet lot. In the next instant, a man stepped out from behind a parked SUV and took a shooter's stance. His target was Conn.

The armed man ignored her as if she weren't even there. His mistake.

No hesitation. No second thoughts. Dawn took her shot which hit the shooter in the upper left chest. He emitted no sound, merely jerked at the impact. His shot had gone wide and hit the vehicle next to Conn and Theo. The wounded man coolly reacquired his target.

Bloody buggering hell. What was he? A cyborg or something? She shot again. This time it was a kill shot. He'd pulled the trigger just as her shot hit him. His shot missed, again hitting the vehicle. The shooter fell to the ground, his weapon falling from his hand. He had to be dead. She hadn't missed. But training—and experience—had her run to check him, leading with her gun, just in case he was playing dead or someone else popped out from between the parked cars.

"Shit, fuck, shit." Conn's curses followed her. "Got you covered, Dawn. Make sure he's out of it."

"Dawn, what the fuck?" Sam roared.

"The guy's dead, luv. Conn, keep the pressure on Theo," she said. "I'll cover my own arse."

If someone else were out there, he hadn't made a move yet.

Her skin still crawled and her gut screamed danger, so she kept searching the shadows.

She stooped and picked up the dead man's weapon with her free hand and then hurried back to cover Conn and Theo.

"Good job, Dawn." Conn's voice was as steady and firm as the pressure he put on Theo's wound. The Dutchman's skin was so white as to be translucent. "You okay?"

"I'm fine. Not my first kill." While she schooled her expression to reflect a calm she didn't feel, her insides were fluttering and her primitive brain was debating as to whether she'd live to be an old lady or not. She'd had this argument with her brain each and every time she'd been in a position to use her weapon. Some day her brain would win and she'd hang up her weapons, stay home, and start collecting cats.

Or live with Sam and have his babies … and collect cats.

That would work also. But today, her primitive self would win. She stroked her forefinger along the side of her gun, centering herself.

"Yeah, sure you are. I'm shaky, too," Conn said. "Sam, Ren, where the fuck are you and our backup? Theo's a few pints low and still bleeding. Jesus, I haven't seen this much blood since Iraq."

Worry for Theo lodged at the back of Dawn's mind as time moved in slow motion. The multitudinous shadows created by the landscape lighting as it filtered around trees, shrubs, and parked cars played tricks on her eyes. Then the crawling sensation elevated to fire ants swarming and stinging her senses.

"Sam? Where are you?" Dawn muttered. "Something's coming. We're sitting ducks here."

"I see you," Sam finally said.

She looked up and found him running out of the valet entrance off the lobby. He looked so big, so strong and furious … worried.

"Be there in a—"

Movement in her peripheral vision. Then she spotted a red dot sweep over Sam's chest.

"Sam, get down!"

Taking aim along the trajectory of the laser targeting scope, Dawn took a shot into the darkness at the same time as Sam took his.

The attacker fell forward into the lighted area of the valet driveway. Both shots had hit, but the downed shooter's curses and jerky motions indicated he was still alive. Still dangerous.

Dawn moved to cover Sam who ran toward the man. The wounded fucker had somehow managed to bring his assault rifle up and around. His target was once again Sam.

Like hell. She took the bloody arsehole out.

Sam shot her a fierce glance. "Good shot, sweetheart." Then he bent over and made sure the man was dead and took his rifle. He slung the weapon over his shoulder and began a car-by-car search of the parked cars for more attackers.

Dawn was tempted to join him, but Conn and Theo still needed her, so she took up her position covering them the best she could.

Finally, Ren came running from the side of the hotel where the parking garage was located. He was accompanied by a large number of Dutch marines and resort security. The reinforcements began securing the area alongside of Sam. Sirens sounded in the distance. She wasn't alone any longer.

Letting out a shaky breath, Dawn sat down, her knees suddenly weak in the aftermath of the intense situation, and relaxed against the side of the SUV. "How's Theo?"

Before Conn could answer, Sam reached her side and pulled her up and into his arms. He squeezed her tightly against him, his face buried in her hair. "God, I couldn't get here fast enough."

"I'm fine." She leaned into his strong, solid body and inhaled his scent, allowing it to soothe her. As she petted his back, her heart rate slowed and the boulder lodged in her throat eased. "It's poor Theo who got hurt. Conn?"

"He's lost a lot of blood." Conn swore. "Bastard went for the heart, but Theo must've turned just enough that the knife missed. But it still did a lot of damage. He should make it if we can get blood in him and get him to a trauma surgeon."

Sam looked down at Theo and grimaced. He spoke into the mike positioned along his jaw, "Ren, where are the fucking medics?"

"They're here." Ren left the searchers and joined them. "Make room." He looked at Conn's hands on Theo's chest. "Jesus, Conn. Is he alive?"

"His pulse is fast and thready," Conn replied. "But he's holding on. Theo and I made a deal: he wouldn't die on me, if I didn't give up on him. So far, thanks to Dawn protecting both our asses, we've managed to stay the course."

Dawn buried her face in Sam's chest. He rubbed her back and whispered against her ear, "You did good. You're done for the night. Ren, Conn, and I will finish this with the help of the locals. Still not sure how MacLean had time to put this all together—"

"These were Benrabi's men. They were in his cabana at the pool." Dawn sighed and let Sam take more of her weight. "Benrabi's relentless when he wants something … and cunning. He and MacLean had to have a basic plan in place to snatch me before they reached the table—and it was highly adaptable. Benrabi did the same when he snatched me right from under my father's nose and embassy security when I was a teen. MacLean must've texted Benrabi's men, telling them that I'd be coming out with Conn."

"Fuckers," Sam muttered, his cheek pressed against hers.

"They'll be scrambling to find another way out of Aruba," Ren said.

"So, now all we have to do is find them," Dawn said.

"No *we* about it," Sam nudged her toward a Land Rover with a Dutch marine, a real one this time, in the driver's seat. "Let us handle tracking Benrabi and MacLean. The sergeant is going to drive you to the estate and stay with you and Keely. There are several other military guards already there."

"Okay." She patted his chest. His voice, his expression, were filled with worry, so she'd let him protect her. Plus, all in all, she'd done a good night's work: won a lot of money, helped get DNA and an identifying voice print on a traitor, and saved Conn and Sam from getting shot. "Keely and I will want to listen in. So keep the com system on."

"You got it, little cat." He leaned over and kissed her deeply. His kiss was cherishing and filled with the promise of a future together. Then he led her to the Land Rover.

Cupping his beard-shadowed jaw, she pulled him down for another kiss. "I think I love you, Sam."

"God, Dawn. I know I love you."

His words resonated and something inside her clicked into place. No more thinking about it—she loved this man, every bleeding dominant, alpha-male centimeter of him.

Sam touched his forehead to hers. "See you later."

"Stay safe," she whispered against his lips.

"I will," he promised.

CHAPTER 13

10: 45 p.m., Orangestad's Port, Aruba

Sam, Ren, and Conn were present on the docks when the kidnapped girls gripping blankets around their scantily clad bodies were taken off several Aruban Coast Guard boats and loaded onto waiting busses. All of them would be taken to the main hospital in Aruba's capital to be checked over.

Since their private yachts had been seized, Benrabi and MacLean couldn't easily escape by water. To make sure the two didn't sneak onto some other docked ship, Sam and the others had helped search the port area, which had been placed on high alert. The Dutch navy, backed up by some U.S. naval ships stationed in Aruba, were stopping and boarding all boats in the waters around Aruba, Bonaire, and Curacao.

The Queen Beatrix airport was on lock-down. Nothing was taking off until the Dutch military said so. The local police with Dutch marines assisting were investigating all private airstrips and helipads. No plane or helicopter had taken off since the shootout in the drive of the hotel as verified by live satellite feed per Keely.

"So, where do we go next?" Sam said.

Ren looked grim. "We may have to have the Aruban police alert the public and then institute a house-by-house search to root the fuckers out."

Sam shook his head in disgust. "MacLean has always been a slippery bastard. We have to stop him here and now, or he'll be in the wind again. And I want Benrabi locked away—far away from Dawn."

"Let me touch base with Keely," Ren said. "She and Dawn might have something for us from the satellite and CCTV feeds she's tapped into." He tapped his com-link. "Keely ... Keely ... Sprite?" His voice had grown frantic with each lack of response. "Fuck. She isn't answering. She always answers."

"Maybe she's taking a bio break." Conn's voice was steady and reasonable.

Ren's growing concern had infected Sam. "They both wouldn't be unreachable. If Keely was in the bathroom, Dawn should've responded. When was the last time we heard from them?"

"At 2230." Ren ran toward the Ranger Rover he, Conn, and Sam were using, shouting over his shoulder. "That's when Keely relayed the all-clear report on the private airstrips."

Keeping pace with Ren, Sam attempted to raise the Dutch marine guards assigned to guard the women. "Fuck it. The guards aren't responding either."

Sam ran and got into the driver's seat. Conn piled into the back passenger seat as Ren rode shotgun. "Hold on." He put the car in gear and accelerated down the port road like a rocket.

"Captain Hoffmann, this is Ren Maddox. No one's answering at my rental." Ren paused, listening, then growled out, "Fuck—"

"What's fuck?" Sam glanced at Ren and found a look on the former SEAL's face that meant the whole situation had just gone FUBAR.

Ren looked at him and waved him off. "Captain, consider the situation as dire. We need backup there, ground and air, ASAP. The escaped criminals plus an unknown number of accomplices have taken over the premises. My wife and Dawn Wilson might be hostages."

Sam snarled and floored the accelerator. Ren shot a fierce glance at him. "Yeah, we're on our way. We'll meet you at the entrance to the road leading to the main house. Out."

"What happened to the guards Hoffmann assigned to our women?" Sam asked as he swerved around slow-moving vehicles on the coastal road.

Ren braced his hand on the dashboard. "His men didn't check in as scheduled at 2230 hours."

"Why in the fuck didn't they send someone to check on them?" Conn's tone was terse.

"They did. Immediately. Those men haven't been heard from either," Ren said. "Hoffmann was ready to send in a helicopter to investigate."

"Jesus, Ren—" Sam growled. "If the girls are being held hostage—the sound of a helicopter might escalate the situation." He didn't want to think about what MacLean might do to the girls to get air surveillance withdrawn.

"Hoffman understands the situation is delicate." Ren let out a harsh breath. "But we need a chopper there in case they attempt to escape with one or both of our women."

"Yeah." Sam glanced at the digital clock on the dashboard. It read 10:50 p.m. "So sometime between the guards' report at 2200 hours and their missed report at 2230, MacLean and Benrabi and an unknown number of men entered the estate and took out the guards, right?"

"Yeah." Ren sounded ice-cold, but the vibes coming off the man were volcanic in their intensity. "We know the girls were okay at 2230 since Keely would've used our code word for trouble if she were being held hostage."

"Let's give the girls credit. They're smart. They'll be alert. They can handle themselves," Conn said. "And, worst case, if they're being held, they'll know we're coming for them and will do what is needed to stay safe."

Yeah, his little cat and Keely were smart and resourceful, but a lot of bad things could happen to the women no matter how well-trained they were. Plus, they'd be out-numbered. Rats always travelled in packs.

"Dammit!" The acidic burn of guilt, helplessness, and fear seared his gut. He'd sent the woman he loved into danger. "Dawn was supposed to be safe." He pushed the Rover up to one hundred miles per hour. The Aruban coastal roads weren't designed for this kind of speed, but fuck it.

As Sam drove like a bat out of hell, he was aware of Ren and Conn checking over their weapons.

———

10:40 pm, Keely and Ren's rental

DAWN STEPPED INTO THE GREAT room, having changed into cut-off jean shorts, a tank top, and a pair of flip-flops. She still wasn't wearing a bra or knickers since she drew the line at wearing another woman's lingerie. Her thigh holster was strapped on one exposed thigh; her gun was loaded with a fresh clip. As long as MacLean and Benrabi were at-large, she wanted a loaded gun within reach.

"Thanks for sharing your wardrobe. I like these clothes much better than that bandage dress you loaned me."

Keely looked up from the computer and smiled. "You can keep the Leger. Ren threatened to beat me daily if I didn't lose it." She giggled. "He loves me naked, not sure why he didn't like the dress."

Dawn sat next to Keely and studied the images on the multiple monitors. "Maybe because you dared to wear it in public … around other men?"

"That was probably it." Keely angled her head and grinned. "I love pulling my macho man's tail. He's so frick-fracking cute when he gets pissed and goes all caveman on me."

"Hmm," Dawn studied her new friend, "so you tempt his beast a lot?"

"Yep, and you should take a leaf from my book and do the same with Sam." Keely patted her hand over her heart. "Makes my heart rate freaking crazy when Ren goes all alpha and spanks my ass. The sex that follows is frick-fracking amazing. Rough, fast, and all night long."

"He spanks you?" Dawn's face grew warm with embarrassment, but a flood of moisture coated her pussy and her clit throbbed at the idea of being spanked before sex.

"Sexy spanking." Keely winked. "I get so hot, so fast, my first orgasm is almost a spontaneous combustion. I have so many orgasms during one of those sessions, my pussy tingles for two days."

Dawn could see Sam giving her that kind of sexual experience. She had a full-body shiver merely thinking about it.

"Isn't that topping from below?" Dawn asked. "Manipulating Ren into getting what you want in bed?"

"Yeah, and my hunk of a man knows it." Keely laughed. "But he likes the results, too."

"I bet." Dawn noticed a shadow on one of the screens displaying the rental estate's grounds. "What's that?" She pointed to an area just off the drive in front of the house. "It wasn't there the last time the camera scanned over the area."

Keely repositioned the camera and zeroed in on the shadow. "Shit, that's a body."

Dawn picked up a walkie-talkie like the one the Dutch marines guarding the house used. "Come in, Nils." No answer. "Johann?" No answer. "Dirk?" No answer.

"Frick-fracking donkey balls." Keely picked up her gun off the computer console and flicked off the safety. Dawn pulled hers from her thigh holster and did the same thing, then re-holstered it.

"Ren? … Come in, big guy." Keely spoke into the SSI headset aligned along her jaw. She switched frequency. "Ren? Conn? … Shit, shit, shit. No signal. Let's go."

Keely only paused long enough to shut down the monitors and to grab her small computer tablet.

Dawn's heart threatened to pound out of her chest as adrenaline flooded into her bloodstream, preparing her for fight or flight. She wasn't sure what Keely was planning, but was certain the woman had a specific end game.

Keely set a fast pace as she led the way into the back of the house and then down the basement stairs. "Why can't we radio out?" Dawn asked.

"Someone's jamming those audio frequencies." Keely's voice was calm; her breathing was only slightly elevated. "Lucky for us, the security video and audio is hardwired, so we'll be able to locate, track, and listen in on the intruders once we reach our safe place. Hold onto me. I don't want to turn on any lights and draw anyone's attention."

As if Keely's words conjured them up, footsteps sounded overhead. Heavy, hard, rapid thuds. Dawn couldn't tell how many, just that there were a lot of them. She bet two of the housebreakers were Benrabi and MacLean. Since she'd been extremely lucky at cards tonight, it was a sure bet.

Keely let out a wispy "ssh" and moved away from the bottom of the dimly lit stairs and into the Stygian darkness of the basement's main room.

Gradually, Dawn's eyes adjusted. They stopped in front of a wine rack-covered wall. Keely pulled out one bottle and a section of the wine racks opened to reveal a door made of what looked to be steel and had a key-pad security lock.

Dawn murmured in a low, non-carrying tone. "In a rental?"

Keely's grin showed white in the relative darkness. Then she turned and entered a code on the pad. The steel door opened into a dark room with only a *whoosh*. They entered and automatic lighting came on.

Keely shut the door and the lock clunked solidly.

They were safe.

Keely moved to a set of security monitors and fired them up. Looking over her shoulder while typing rapidly, she said, "This is why we rented the place. It's owned by a wanna-be dictator from one of the Mexican coastal states. He's very security conscious."

"You mean this house is owned by a drug cartel leader?" Dawn said. She didn't know who else would have the audacity to want to be a dictator in Mexico.

"Yep. But he's in jail right now," muttered Keely as she typed on the security system key board, pulling up camera feeds and reprogramming the cameras to do whatever it is the small computer genius wanted them to do. "So he doesn't need it. His estate manager was happy to take money under the table. What El Jefe doesn't know won't hurt him. Ahh, there you are, you frick-fracking douchebags."

Dawn looked over Keely's shoulder. MacLean, Benrabi, and some of the biggest, ugliest thugs she'd ever seen in her life stood in the great room she and Keely had just vacated. The men looked around and appeared to be angry their quarry had managed to escape them.

Yay for Team Keely and Dawn.

"Can you get audio on those cameras?" Dawn asked.

"That's what I'm working on," Keely replied, a pissed tone in her voice. "Darn it, El Jefe was an el cheapo. No wonder he always gets caught when he hides out at his properties. His system needs a new sound card for the upgraded software I downloaded when we arrived. Okay, this is the best I can do."

"Where … they…?" Static cut out some of Benrabi's words. "…perimeter … no … contact."

Perimeter?

"Bollocks, they have even more men outside." Dawn looked at Keely. "Can you pull up the outside cameras?"

Keely nodded and displayed multiple exterior feeds on the monitor array, then began keying in commands while muttering to herself.

Dawn peered at the outside video images as they appeared while trying to decipher what the bleeding hell Benrabi and MacLean were saying.

MacLean spoke, "Armando … search … here somewhere—"

Keely muttered, "Woot! Fixed it." The audio feed cleared up and MacLean's words were now crystal-clear.

"—look under beds and in closets. They're small women and could hide where a child might."

Several men ran off.

"Child?" Keely sounded pissed. "Did he just compare us to children? What a frick-fracking jerk. I'll show him who's a child when I gut his ass." She angled her head toward a large case on a chair. "Ren and I brought some extra toys…"

Dawn opened the case and laughed with delight. "Ooh, mine." She pulled out a really nice blade with its own sheath and strapped it to her other thigh. Like Angelina Jolie in *Tomb Raider*, she now had a weapon on each thigh.

Going back into the case, she cooed, "Oh, look, a dart gun." She gave Keely a thumbs up. "Just what I need for the silent take-down of bleeding arseholes."

Strapping on a bum bag, Dawn placed the dart gun, a supply of tranquilizer darts, and an extra clip for her gun and some bullets for a reload, if needed, inside it. "It's like Christmas and my birthday all rolled into one, and the only better gift would be to tell me there's a back way out of this room so I can go outside and play pin the dart on the arseholes in the garden with my trusty dart gun."

Keely giggled. "Like an Aruban version of *Clue*. You'll be delighted to know there is." She pushed a button on the desk.

To their left, a door slid open, revealing a tunnel with LED floor lighting.

"While you go and litter the landscaping with bodies, I'll use the land-line and call the Aruban national police and have them patch me through to Ren."

Dawn frowned, her hands planted on her hips. "Why didn't you call first thing? When our military guards didn't report into their headquarters on time, all hell probably broke loose. Our men are probably racing here and will walk into a trap."

"Bull-hockey." Keely picked up an old rotary dial Princess phone and dialed 911 for police emergency. "Our men aren't stupid. They know we'll do the smart thing until they get here."

"Well, I should hope so. But still, please let them know we're all right as soon as possible. Sam's got to be going stark raving bonkers." Dawn looked at Keely's tablet. "Will I be able to see the outside camera feeds on that tablet of yours?"

"Yes." Keely pulled up a screen and then handed it to her. "The red icons are the camera locations. Tap on one and you'll see the live feed. You can use night vision or not, depending on the area lighting. The cameras also have infrared sensors." She demonstrated how to switch between night-vision to infrared and back.

"All the mod cons. Thanks." Dawn put the tablet into sleep mode to dim the screen after locating her first target's exact position.

"Be careful," Keely said. "I'll try to work around their audio jammer, so put on one of the headsets."

Dawn snagged one out of the case and put it on, making sure it was ready to receive.

"I'll contact you once I get the com system working again." Keely cursed at the phone she held to her ear and disconnected, then dialed "0" this time. "God, the frick-fracking emergency line is busy. Um, operator … yes, police emergency… yeah, I'll hold."

Keely looked at Dawn and fluttered her hand. "Shoo. Go. Take out bad guys. Then get your ass back here PDQ so Sam doesn't kill me for putting you in danger."

Dawn snorted. "I'll be careful, mum."

Keely shot Dawn a middle finger as she spoke into the phone, "Yes, I'm still here. Don't you people understand what a frick-fracking emergency means?"

Moving into the tunnel, Dawn made her way up and out. She could smell the ocean on the night air, which was still warm from the heat of the day, and the exotic blooms from the formal gardens surrounding the house. El Jefe, whoever the fuck he was, had a lot of money to waste on watering subtropical rain forest plants in what was a subtropical desert climate.

The escape tunnel exited behind an artfully designed rock wall that was further camouflaged by Jacaranda shrubs in full bloom. Dawn paused. While still hidden in the shadows of the tunnel opening, she sheltered the tablet's screen with her body and rechecked the guards' positions.

Her first target hadn't moved and was only ten meters away, by the pool house. The dumb ass was smoking a cigarette. Even if she hadn't seen his image on infrared, she would've smelled the smoke as it wafted on the light breeze. She wrinkled her nose against the pungent scent that smelled like camel dung.

Sliding the tablet into her bum bag, she pulled out the dart gun and loaded one dart and tucked an extra one into her knife sheath. She stalked her prey, using the abundant foliage and shadows to cover her approach. Every sense on high alert, she pictured every possible thing that could go wrong and how she'd counteract the situation if something did. The worst-case-scenario would be if the tranquilizer didn't work quickly and the man cried out. She needed to get close enough so she could cover his mouth as he went down.

Risky? Yes. But she didn't want him shouting and bringing his mates into the mix.

As she approached, the low-level lighting in the pool area gave off enough light for her to see the guard clearly. Stopping behind a large fern about three meters away, she waited for a second or two to see if the man had heard her approach. He didn't move and continued to act as if he were on vacation rather than guard duty. His assault rifle was carelessly slung across his back. His focus was straight-ahead— and on his cigarette.

All in all, she wasn't impressed with the first of Benrabi's security guards. If the others were this lax, she'd be back in the safe room in no time.

Don't get cocky, Dawn. All the cocky bitches get killed in the movies.

Just as she was about to move from behind the fern and take the smoking guard down, he received a call over his radio. His Arabic wasn't a dialect she recognized, but she got enough of the gist to know this was a routine report and he wouldn't be missed for a while after she took him out. Her lucky streak was still going strong.

From the outside camera feeds, as far as she could tell, there were only four exterior guards. If she could neutralize them, her Marine, Ren, and Conn would have a cake walk in their infiltration of the estate. She had no doubt they were already on their way, so she needed to get to work.

The guard clicked off his radio and resumed smoking. She tip-toed behind him and when she was less than a meter away, she took aim and shot him in the neck. He inhaled sharply, reached for the dart, and then dropped to the ground.

She'd have to compliment Ren for buying a highly potent tranquilizer. Still, she was cautious when she bent over to make sure the man was completely out.

His breathing was slow and he didn't react when she touched him. Luckily for her, he had a couple of sets of flex-cuffs which she used to restrain his hands and ankles, then she used his headdress to gag him. She removed a knife she found and hid it under some bushes with his rifle. Before she left him, she ground his still-burning cigarette under the heel of her flip-flops.

One down, three to go.

She reloaded the dart gun, then checked the tablet and moved to the next unsuspecting prey by the garage area.

Chapter 14

Sam pulled the Rover into a driveway less than fifty yards away from the entrance to the private road leading to the rental. He turned to Ren, "What's the plan?"

"God, I love my wife." Ren grinned like a loon as he swiped off a call he'd received mere seconds ago on his phone.

"Hell, we know that, man," Sam said, "but she's in danger. Why are you smiling?"

"She and Dawn noticed their guards were down so they went to the safe room in the basement before the house was breached. They're okay." Ren laughed. "There's no way those fuckers can get into that safe room. The drug lord who owns the estate built it to withstand WWIII and the zombie apocalypse. Plus, I also stocked the room with some extra weapons, just in case."

"Thank fuck." Dawn was safe. Sam turned to high-five Conn who sported a shit-eating grin on his face. "That means we can go hunting without the girls getting caught in the crossfire."

"Um, well, not quite." Ren's voice wasn't quite as exuberant as before. "Our gals aren't sitting on their so-fine tushes, waiting for their men to rescue them."

A sick feeling hit Sam in the gut. "Where are their tushes … exactly?"

Ren gripped Sam's shoulder and squeezed. "Keely's in the safe room monitoring Benrabi, MacLean, and five other men as they search the house. She's blocking them from accessing any of the estate camera feeds and trying to take down their audio jammer so she can feed us intel directly." He sighed. "But Dawn's sneaking around outside, eliminating bad guys so we don't waltz into a clusterfuck."

"Shit … fuck … damn." Sam hit the steering wheel with each curse, before stopping to take in Conn and Ren's commiserating, but somewhat amused expressions. "She didn't think two former spec ops Marines and one Navy SEAL could handle a bunch of third-world tangos and a former DIA desk jockey?"

"Guess not, buddy." Conn patted him on the shoulder. "Let's go see what your little woman has left us to do."

After one more muttered curse, Sam exited the driver's side. He ran to the back of the vehicle to meet up with Ren and Conn. The three of them pulled out body armor and weapons and swiftly loaded themselves up.

"We'll head for the outside entrance to the safe room," Ren said. "Keely said by the time we get there, Dawn should be back inside. She's tranquilizing the perimeter guards and then cuffing them."

Sam heard the respect for Dawn's actions in Ren's voice. Damn, his woman was a warrior, and he'd be sure to let her know how proud he was of her … once she was safely snuggled in his arms.

They set off for the estate at a quick jog. As they made their way toward the back of the sprawling house, they ran across two of the guards Dawn had taken down. They were semi-conscious, bound hand-and-foot, gagged with pieces of their own clothing, and disarmed.

Conn shot Sam a wide grin.

Sam shook his head and chuckled silently. Yeah, Dawn would've made a damn good spec ops Marine.

Ren gave them a hand signal to hold up, then he scouted ahead. Sam and Conn hunkered down in a grouping of ornamental shrubs. A few seconds later, a low whistle told them to come ahead. They met up with the SSI boss by some flowering bushes.

They moved behind the foliage and confronted what looked to be a rock wall. Ren opened a small door camouflaged as part of the rock to reveal a key pad. He entered a code and a door slid open and led into a LED-floor-lit tunnel that sloped downwards. Entering the tunnel, Sam and Conn followed as Ren led. The door behind them slid shut with only a change of air pressure to indicate its closing.

Less than two minutes later, they entered a room with beds, supplies, and a computer array that would make NSA proud. Keely was in the center of it all, the mistress of all she surveyed.

"Sprite," Ren called out. Keely jumped up and ran to her husband.

"Where's Dawn?" Sam asked Keely.

"Still outside. She had one guy left at the end of the driveway."

"Fuck." Sam walked over and looked at the camera images, switching to infrared to spot human heat patterns more easily. He spotted Dawn's small figure as she used the landscaping to cover her approach to a guard. He admired her stealthy approach.

"They are not in the house. MacLean can waste time inside if he wishes." Benrabi's accented voice came over the audio feed.

Sam hunted for and found Benrabi and another man on a camera image as they exited the front door of the house.

"Our men are not answering us," Benrabi continued. "The infidel bitches must have gotten to them. Outside is where we'll find the whores."

"Fuck." Sam turned and headed for the tunnel. "I'm going out to backup Dawn. Then we'll come back and help y'all with MacLean and the rest of them."

"Hell, buddy," Conn said. "If Ren and I can't handle the other assholes, then we might as well retire and watch soap operas and eat bonbons."

——

ON ADRENALINE-OVERLOAD, EVERY MUSCLE IN DAWN's body was tight with tension and the strain of having cuffed and pulled three large men's bodies into the shadows. Her breathing was overly rapid and she was hyper-alert to every noise and movement around her.

Leaning against a palm tree, Dawn used the trunk to block the light from the tablet and rechecked the position of the last guard. He was secreted in a small grouping of ferns by the entrance to the long driveway leading to the house. She only had cover for about four meters of the twenty meter distance between them.

Checking over the dart pistol, she took off her holsters and placed them under a bush, then she tucked her gun into the bum bag and placed the dart gun into the waistband at the back of her shorts. She rubbed some dirt over her arms and legs and disheveled her hair. Then she ripped her tank top so that one strap was torn and the front of the shirt revealed far too much of one pale breast.

Faking a limp, she hobbled down the road toward the man whose gaze was fixed in the direction of the main road and not scanning his surroundings as a more expert guard should be doing.

Where did Benrabi get these jokers? Guards 'R Us?

When she was about two meters away, she stopped, bent over, and wheezed as if she were out of breath. She braced her dominant hand on her back, just above the grip of the dart gun.

"Help me! Please," she panted out, keeping a sharp eye on the man.

He stepped out of the shadows into the light cast by one of a series of ornamental light posts lining the drive. Bringing his submachine pistol up, he aimed it at her.

"Come here, woman." His accent was thick, not Yemeni. Maybe Syrian.

Dawn straightened somewhat, but kept her hand on her back as if she was in pain, and then moved forward with an exaggerated limp.

The man's expression showed no fear—and no suspicion of her at all. She was, after all, a mere woman, harmless and needing a man to direct her every action.

Yeah, you just keep thinking I'm harmless, you fuckwit.

He moved forward, his weapon now aimed at the ground. His gaze was fixed on her naked breast, which had fallen completely out of her top as she moved. He had an unholy gleam in his eyes.

Was the twatface salivating? He was.

Anger flowed through her veins like molten lava. In one fluid move, she pulled the dart gun, brought it around, and shot him in the throat. The shocked expression on his face as he fell face down on the pea-gravel drive made her happy.

She shoved the dart gun into her back waistband and rushed forward. Checking his belt and his pockets, she couldn't find a single, bleeding flex cuff on his person.

Luckily, she had an extra set she'd taken off one of the other guards. She cuffed his hands behind his back and then used his own knife to cut his shirt into pieces and gagged him. She tossed his gun into a run-off ditch alongside the drive, then turned to head back to the safe room tunnel entrance.

"Bitch!"

The speaker came around a curve in the driveway and ran straight at her. It was Benrabi and the man MacLean had called Armando was on his heels.

She barely managed to twist away from Benrabi's grasping hands. She swiped at him with the downed guard's knife she still held in her hand and caught the sheikh's arm. He roared in pain and anger, but before he could grab her, he tripped over the guard she'd just felled.

Armando moved toward her, slowly, inexorably, with an evil leer on his face. He was huge. His large hands probably could break her in two as easily as most men could snap a twig.

Shifting the knife into her non-dominant hand, she moved away from Armando and the cursing Benrabi, back into the landscaping along the driveway. She kept the knife pointed at Armando, warding him off as she used her other hand to pull the dart gun from her waistband.

Bloody buggering hell. She kept her hand behind her back. The dart gun was empty and her handgun was in the zipped bum bag. She couldn't load the dart gun and hold the knife at the same time or unzip the bum bag with one hand. So she dropped the knife.

Armando looked at the knife lying on the ground and laughed.

Dawn pulled an extra dart from a back pocket in her shorts.

"Come to me, *puta*." Armando crooked a finger at her. "I promise I won't hurt you."

The man was confident that she was the prey and he, the predator. Yeah, right, and the Queen was a Yank.

Still backing away and with both hands behind her back, Dawn loaded the dart gun by feel. She'd done it enough this evening that she had the process down. She kept her eyes on Armando and Benrabi who now struggled to his feet.

"Bitch, you cut me." Growling like a wild beast, Benrabi stood, a gun in his hand. He pointed it at her.

She dove for a small grassy ditch just as he shot.

Either his aim was off or he'd intended to shoot her in the leg. The bullet creased her thigh.

"Bloody hell!" Dawn hit the grassy berm and rolled down a slight slope. When she stopped rolling, she was on her back in the shallow ditch. She had managed to hold onto the dart gun and brought it up and shot Benrabi in the face as he dove at her with a bellow.

The dart lodged in the soft tissue of his cheek. She had an up close and personal view of her marksmanship since he'd fallen on top of her before she could move out of the way. His gross, smelly bulk now covered her from head-to-toe like an obscene lover from hell.

"Fucking arsehole weighs a fucking ton." She gasped, trying to catch a full breath—and not succeeding. She wiggled and shoved and wasted what little oxygen she had, but couldn't budge the arsebadger at all. She needed to get out from under him, because she was seeing spots—evidence she could lose consciousness soon—and Armando was still a danger.

Suddenly the air thickened like a thunderstorm was about to break. The atmosphere was so dense, so charged with electricity, she found it even harder to breathe. Or maybe that was because the arsehole Benrabi was compressing her diaphragm.

Danger was definitely coming. It had to be Armando, stalking her, prolonging the threat, making her wait before he pounced. Shit, she couldn't get to her gun or even reload the dart gun, which was still in her hand, because that arm was pinned down by the ape on top of her.

Bleeding hell. She renewed her efforts to shift Benrabi off her.

Then a roar rent the silence of the night. "Dawn!"

Was she dreaming? That sounded like Sam.

Pounding feet approached her position from the direction of the safe room tunnel.

Armando leaned down to pull Benrabi off her. He'd use her as a hostage, but he didn't get the chance.

"Motherfucker," Sam yelled and Armando's face disappeared from her sight.

Thud. Thwap. Grunts. Groans. Sam was fighting to protect her and she could do nothing to help him. She struggled to get out from under Benrabi or at least move him enough so she could see what was happening.

And then there was silence, heavy and thick, broken only by rapid, harsh breaths.

"Sam ... luv..." she cried out.

"I'm fine, sweetheart."

His words brought tears to her eyes. Benrabi's bulk was torn away and she took a deep breath of glorious air. Then she winced as her ribs protested the sudden, violent expansion of her lungs.

"Sweetheart? You hurt?" Sam knelt by her prone body. With his gun in one hand and aimed at Benrabi—he used his free hand to check over her limbs, testing joints with a competent, gentle touch.

"I'm all right." She panted like an exhausted puppy. She smiled at his concerned face, backlit by the lights lining the driveway. "Thanks ... getting ... arsehole off. Stop ... fussing. Benrabi won't ... unconscious ... for long. Armando..."

Sam leaned over and kissed her silent, giving her his breath. "Armando's dead. If Benrabi moves, he's dead. Now, lie still and let me take care of you, little warrior." He blew out a breath and leaned his forehead against her. "You did good, little cat. You can partner me on an op any day—God ... sweetheart ... I sent you away and put you in danger. Forgive..."

"Shut it, luv. You did what you felt was right." She soothed the muscle pulsing along his jaw line with her thumb. "Like a good partner, you were here when I needed you. I'm fine."

"*Meneer* Crocker?" A man with a Dutch accent called out.

"Over here, Captain Hoffmann." Sam turned and smiled down at her. "The Dutch marines have arrived."

"Better late, then never, right?" She returned his smile.

"Does the *jongedame* need medical attention?" Captain Hoffmann asked as he loomed over them. Behind the Dutchman, other marines took control of Benrabi and checked over Armando's body.

"No," Dawn said then winced when Sam began palpating her ribs.

"Yes, she does," Sam said. "The fucker bruised, maybe cracked some of your ribs." Her Marine moved to block her body with his as he tied her torn top so that her breast was covered. His narrowed glance went to her shorts and some of the tension in his body released when he saw her shorts were intact.

"Just bruised, luv," she said in a reassuring, soothing tone since her man was balanced on the fine edge of putting Benrabi down. "A few anti-inflammatories and I'll be right as rain." She caressed his face. "So relax. I'm fine." She looked around. "Where's Ren and Conn? Keely's back at the…"

"Shh. Ren and Conn are back at the house, taking out the rest of the bad asses, and Keely is, hopefully, staying put in the safe room."

Dawn struggled to rise. "We should go help them."

"We aren't going anywhere. You've done your job, little warrior." Sam placed a hand on her arm and lowered her back to the soft grass of the ditch. He ran his hand down her side and then froze and raised his hand—covered in her blood.

Shit, she'd forgotten Benrabi had tagged her. She aimed a nasty glance at the fuckwit, who glared at her. "Benrabi's conscious. He's a fucking fast metabolizer."

"Fuck his metabolism. You're bleeding." Sam growled and took the small flashlight Captain Hoffmann handed him and aimed it at her thigh. The Dutchman looked grim. Her Marine looked killing mad.

"Hey, I got the wanker back. I knifed and then darted him. In all the action and him falling on me, I sort of forgot he shot me." She petted Sam's arm. "It's a crease. Nothing major involved. Just some fat."

Sam snapped. "If you're bleeding, you're not fucking fine. You're a mess, baby. Your top was torn—did the fucker hurt you anywhere else you're not telling me about?" He began checking over her hips again as if his earlier look had missed something.

"Sam, luv, I dirtied myself up and tore my top to distract the guard." She petted him wherever she could touch him. "That's all that happened. I promise."

Dawn looked at Sam and then Captain Hoffmann. "Someone needs to go help Ren and Conn so Keely can come out of the safe room."

"I'm not leaving you," Sam said. "Captain, would…"

"It is done, *Meneer* Crocker. Stay with your woman." The Captain smiled at her. "You ever want to join the Dutch marines, *Juffrouw*, I would be proud to have you in my unit." He saluted her and went to join his men, shouting orders.

"You aren't joining the Royal Dutch Marines, little warrior," Sam said with a growl in his voice. "I'm quitting the CIA and joining SSI to partner with you."

"Bossy man." Dawn laughed and winced at the pain in her ribs.

Sam snarled and placed a gentle hand over her ribs. Then he yelled over his shoulder, "I need a medic." He carefully gathered her into his arms and stood with her cradled tenderly against his chest.

"Sam, put me dow—" Her demand was cut off by his kiss.

"Don't argue with your man. I'm carrying you. You're getting checked over by a medic. Even if you're merely bruised, your wound needs to be cleaned and bandaged."

Her Marine's temper was on shaky ground. Time to humor him and let him care for her.

"Okay, luv." She snuggled her head on his shoulder. "Can I get something to drink? Taking out arseholes is thirsty work."

"A drink coming right up." He rubbed his cheek over her hair. He blew out a choppy breath. "God … I thought I was going to lose you, Dawn. When I saw Benrabi on top of you … I was more scared than I've ever been in my life."

"I was fine, luv. I was worried about you and the guys heading into a trap. I had to do something." Dawn touched Sam's face and tipped his chin so she could look him in his eyes. She winced at the fear that lingered in his beautiful grey eyes. She traced the grim line of his lips with the tip of a very dirty finger. He kissed it.

"You were more than fine, sweetheart." Sam nibbled her finger. "You were a fucking Amazon warrior."

"Amazon, luv? I might need to grow a foot or two to meet that description."

"My Amazon warrior." He sucked her finger into his mouth.

"Sam … my finger's dirty. Don't kiss it," she scolded.

He let her finger slip from his mouth and husked, "I don't fucking care. I want to strip you down and then touch and kiss every inch of you, but I'll wait until you've been cleared by a doctor. Until then, your finger"—he kissed it again—"your lips"—he kissed her mouth—"your face"—he peppered kisses over her face—"are all mine."

Sam tucked her head on his shoulder. "Little warrior, I said it earlier and it's worth repeating … I'm so damn proud of what you did tonight. So honored you're my woman. But the next time we go into battle, we're sticking to each other like glue, that way I won't get five years scared off my life."

"Luv, did you mean what you said earlier?" She raised her head and held his gleaming silver gaze with hers.

"What's that, baby?" he asked.

"Are you quitting the CIA and coming to work for Ren?" She held her breath. It was what she wanted, but she'd never force him to leave the CIA if he wanted to stay.

"Yeah. I meant it. If Ren will have me, and he's hinted he would. You okay with that?""Yes." She brushed a kiss over his lips. "Very okay." She teased him with another light kiss.

Sam stopped walking toward the medic's van and opened his mouth. She took the invitation and kissed him more fully, sliding her tongue into his mouth. He returned the kiss, eating at her mouth gently, showing her his love, his need for her.

Dawn pulled away and placed little kisses along his jaw line. "I love you, Sam Crocker. And when you go all Neanderthal on me, I'll forgive you since I know you're protecting me because you love me. Just as I'll protect you, because I love you. We Amazon warriors don't let anyone mess with our men."

"Fuck me, I'm so lucky." He looked at her, a twisted grin on his face and an expression in his eyes that made her heart melt and her eyes tear. "I love you, Dawn Wilson, my little cat, my little warrior. You're gonna marry me—soon—and I'll spend the rest of my life making sure you never walk into trouble alone again."

Dawn cradled his face between her palms and whispered against his lips. "Such a good partner you are, Sam Crocker, my Marine."

Epilogue

Later that night, Ren and Keely's rental

Sam sat with Dawn cuddled on his lap on a couch in the great room. The patio doors were open and the early morning breeze off the ocean felt good. Ren, Keely and Conn were also present. The five of them had just finished eating a late night or early morning, depending on how you looked at it, meal. The gals had thrown the food together after the Dutch military, the Aruban police, and the Commander of the U.S. Navy's Aruban base had left after a short debriefing.

No one had been to sleep yet. But Sam doubted any of them would have been able to sleep. The adrenaline had yet to wear off for any of them.

Keely sitting on Ren's lap was telling Sam and Dawn about what had gone on in the house while Sam had gone after Dawn. "So, when Ren spotted MacLean on the video feed, he turned to me and growled—"

"I did not growl." Ren idly played with his wife's blonde curls.

"Yes, you did," Keely insisted.

"Ah, Ren, you did," Conn said, his lips twisted into a grin.

Ren glared at Conn. "Whose side are you on?"

"Keely's—'cause you growled," Conn said. "Well, it might have been a snarl. Same difference."

Keely shot Conn a grin. "Thanks, Conn. Anywho —where in the frick-fracking hell did I leave off?" She frowned at her husband who laughed and kissed the tip of her scrunched nose.

Sam laughed then prompted, "Ren saw MacLean on the feed and he growled at you."

"Oh, yeah." Keely gave Sam's a thumbs up. "I'm so tired I don't know why I'm still awake." She yawned then laid her head on her husband's shoulder. "Anywho. Ren told me forcefully to stay put. Said that he and Conn could handle the frick-fracking riff-raff. Well, he used other words, most of them some form of the f-word or another, but you get the idea."

Dawn giggled. Sam kissed the top of her head which was nestled on his chest. She was a sweet, warm armful and he was a lucky bastard.

"So, did you stay put?" Dawn asked.

"No, she did not," snarled Ren. "She waited a few minutes and followed us."

"And it was a good thing she did," Conn said. He looked over at him and Dawn. "She saved me a serious injury by taking out a guy who'd come up on my back while I was occupied with another fucker." He sent a Keely a grateful look.

Ren kissed his wife's forehead and cuddled her more tightly against his body. "Yeah, she can be useful." Keely pinched his forearm. "Okay, you're a great asset, though I could've done without all your shouted encouragement while I beat on MacLean."

"Hey, I was doing some shouting of my own, Ren," Conn said. "That had to be one of the best beat-downs I've seen in a long while—well, for a Navy man."

Sam laughed and winked at Conn. "Yeah, Dawn and I came in on the end of that fight. Shit, boss, you could've made the cut in my and Conn's Marine spec ops unit."

Ren growled and threw a couch pillow at Sam who protected Dawn from getting hit by batting it away.

"Sorry, Dawn," Ren said. "Wasn't trying to hit you. Just that jarhead you're using as a chair."

Dawn giggled like a little kid. Sam couldn't resist stealing a kiss and absorbing the joy coming from her into his very soul.

After the kiss, Dawn laid her head back on his chest and turned toward the others who had been silent and highly interested observers. "So, what's going to happen with MacLean and Benrabi?" She yawned. "Keely and I were slaving over a hot microwave while you men were talking to the authorities."

"MacLean is in the brig on one of the U.S. Naval ships until the DIA can send someone to take him back to the States where he'll be held until he's tried as a traitor. He'll never see the light of day again," Ren said.

"Don't you Yanks still have the death penalty for traitors?" Dawn asked.

"Yeah. He's gonna die eventually," Sam said, a lot of satisfaction in his voice.

"And Benrabi?" Dawn shivered and Sam rubbed her back, soothing her.

"The Dutch have him in custody while several countries are fighting over extraditing him," Ren said. "We can link him to Daesh, or ISIS as it is more commonly known. He's wanted for some terrorist acts he was the architect of. He may be going to France. But the United States is also trying to connect him to the explosion on a naval base in Texas. Keely's making that case for Homeland Security."

Keely glowered. "Benrabi's going down, and he'll do it in the United States or my name isn't Keely Walsh-Maddox."

"My father can help. I'm sure MI6 has intel you can use," Dawn offered. She looked up at Sam. "We can ask him personally when Sam and I fly to England so he can meet my parents."

"*After* we get married first," Sam said. "I'm not taking any chances he won't accept me as a son-in-law."

"Sam-m-m," Dawn drawled.

"Marriage first. Parents after." He kissed the tip of her nose. "I don't want to wait."

Ren coughed and Keely shushed him. Conn just smiled. Sam didn't care that he sounded impatient, but if Dawn wasn't on board, well—

"Oh all right, but—" Dawn caressed the side of his face. "Let's try marriage first. Honeymoon, second. Then meet my parents."

"Deal. What a good partner you are," he said against her lips. "I love you."

"I love you more." She teased the seam of his mouth with the tip of her tongue.

"Impossible," Sam murmured. "But I'm open to being convinced."

~THE END~

CHAPTER ONE

Iguazu River, Argentina, the Triple Frontier

Keely Walsh stopped to rest. Even with the shade from the rain forest canopy, the heat was oppressive. Tipping back her broad-brimmed hat, she wiped the sweat out of her eyes, then took a deep drink of water from the canteen she carried. So far, according to her portable GPS, she'd traveled two klicks from her landing site. If her coordinates were correct, and they always were, she should see the village in less than another kilometer. Right now all she could see were trees, low-growing foliage, and more trees.

After she'd landed the chopper in a small, elevated clearing, she'd followed a faint path leading down and away from the landing site. She surmised the path had been cleared a day or so ago, then just as quickly overgrown. It led in the general direction of the village. She'd seen marijuana growing in the clearing, so it made sense the locals would need a path to get to their cash crop.

Shrugging her backpack off, she let it slip to the ground. She knelt and pulled out the white cotton shirt she'd worn on the plane, then put it on over her tank top. It was way too hot and humid for any covering, but she couldn't have her brother go nuts if he saw the bruises on her shoulders and upper chest. Time enough for explanations later, after they were safe in the hotel suite she'd booked in the Iguazu National Park before securing transportation and her weapons. She sighed, imagining how good the air conditioning would feel after this steam-bath hike. The hotel had a pool and a pool bar. She could almost taste a large Pepsi with ice as she dangled her legs in the cool water.

God, she hated heat, humidity, insects and snakes, all of which jungles had in abundance. Only for her favorite brother, Stuart "Tweeter" Walsh, would she do this—plus there had been no one else. Her father, Marine Corps Colonel Kennard Walsh, was on a training mission. The call to her other four brothers had not produced the instant response needed. The twins, Loren and Paul, were on a SEAL mission and the other two, Devin and Andy, were Marines searching Afghanistan's caves for terrorists. By the time their emergency leave was approved, Tweeter would be dead. And she couldn't trust anyone else but her mother Molly—and her Dad would kill her if she involved her mama in this mess.

She was it—the only person who could warn her brother about the trap. She couldn't stay safely in Massachusetts while Tweeter was in danger. He'd protected her over the years, and she could do no less for him.

She let the shirt tails hang over her baggy khakis. She slid the knife she'd bought from a wizened little man named Bazon in Puerto Iguazu into its sheath, then clipped it and the holster holding the Bren Ten she'd purchased onto the belt at the small of her back. Nothing like a Bren to make your point. She'd taken the finding of the rare gun as a sign that her mission would be a success. There'd only been fifteen hundred made and the odds were astronomical against her finding the gun she was most comfortable handling. Her dad had taught her to shoot with a Bren. It was highly accurate and had hitting power. She checked the magazine and found it fully loaded with all ten .45 caliber rounds. She locked the hammer back to the "condition one" setting; a flick of the safety and she would be good to go for single shot or automatic fire.

Satisfied she was as ready as she could be, she headed once more in the direction of the village where Tweeter, along with his Security Specialist International team, were allegedly meeting an informant.

SSI was a security firm specializing in international troubleshooting for private corporations and governments who would rather not use their own intelligence personnel. Ren and Trey Maddox, both ex-special forces, had established their headquarters and training facility in Sanctuary, Idaho, a SSI-owned town at the edge of the Nez Perce National Forest. SSI's current mission had been arranged through the U.S. Department of Defense and the National Clandestine Service or NCS; the classified report she'd come across while working on a project for the government had outlined the mission as an information-gathering on a reputed al Qaeda organization operating out of the Argentinian section of the Triple Frontier.

What it really was? A specially designed trap for Ren Maddox and anyone who accompanied him.

If the trap hadn't been sprung by the time she made it to the meeting place, they'd hoof it out and head for the helicopter she'd also rented from Bazon. In the Triple Frontier, it was easy to find weapons and drugs—and to rent military-equipped helicopters. She hadn't asked the old man where he'd gotten the Kamov KA-60, kitted out with belly guns and air-to-ground missiles. She never looked gift battle-ready helicopters in the mouth.

Bazon even had ordnance for the belly guns. For double the rental price, she'd had him load the ordnance, checking his work as he did it. She might not be able to lift the ammunition, but she knew how it should be loaded.

She'd been surprised when the man hadn't tried to gyp her. When she'd asked him about it, he'd given her a mostly toothless smile and said, "For you, *pequena muchacha de oro*, it is a pleasure." Then Bazon had winked at her, and his flirtatious manner had her choking back laughter. The Argentinian had to be old enough to be her grandfather.

It probably hadn't hurt that she'd paid him five thousand USD in traveler's checks. Say what you want about the economy and international relations, the almighty dollar was still the currency of choice in the world's hellholes.

Now, if the trap had been sprung—well, she'd cross that bridge when she got to it.

To this point, her trek had been merely hot and sweaty, but not dangerous. She'd seen no one other than monkeys, toucans, butterflies and other inhabitants of this particular subtropical rainforest. Nothing, not even the local four-legged predators, had bothered her. She was more worried about chancing across the two-legged variety before she reached the village. As her father had drilled into her and the boys, "always expect perimeter guards when approaching a danger zone". Since her father had survived some of the hairiest conflicts on the planet and taught thousands of other Marines to pull through in some of the worst places in the world, he knew of what he spoke.

Keely's gaze now moved continuously, watching for anything out of place. She attempted to differentiate the background noises, hoping she'd sense a change when peril approached. The jungle fauna were nature's version of an early-warning system.

When danger did appear, it was on the path. Or, more explicitly, lying across it. She stopped, her steel-toed hiking boots just inches away from a trip wire strung across the path. Was the trap for those stupid enough to steal the villagers' marijuana crop? Or, had it been placed there more recently by the mercs hired to take out the SSI team?

She knelt and examined the wire. She snorted. It went nowhere and was attached to nothing. A red herring. Somewhere around here was the real trap.

She lifted her head and swept the area around the path and a few feet ahead. Ahh, there it was. A disturbed area, no new vegetation had grown, so the digging was recent. After the wary traveler stepped over the more obvious wire, the poor unsuspecting sap would then step onto a pressure plate and die before he or she even finished congratulating themselves on a narrow escape.

Keely couldn't leave the trap for some hapless villager or for her and the guys to stumble over on the return trip to the chopper. Looking around, she spied a pile of rocks. Stepping off the path, she carefully picked her way toward the outcropping, which looked to be the remnants of a small building. She edged around the rubble, picked up a rock, then lobbed it with an underhanded toss. It hit the plate just as she ducked for cover. The explosion was loud, startling birds and other animals into heading for shelter higher in the rain forest canopy. The sound of detritus hitting the broken-down hovel told her it had been a fragmentation mine.

Crouching back under the cover of some low-growing palms, she waited. After the explosion, the sound of silence was pregnant with tension. It was as if the animals of the forest remained silent just as she did, waiting to see who would respond to the mine's destruction.

She just hoped whoever investigated would look, see no body parts, and leave. She wasn't up for killing anyone else this trip just to get to the village. She could kill if she had to—and had recently done so in self-defense—but it had cost her a piece of her soul. Her stomach clenched, acid roiling at the memory. Taking deep breaths, she conquered her nausea, then shoved the images of two men with broken necks, lying in a dirty warehouse in Boston, to a dark corner of her mind.

At the start of this hastily thrown-together trip to South America, she'd thought she could get to the SSI team and let them handle any dirty work. Arming herself was one thing, using her weapons was entirely another. She shook her head in disgust at her naïveté. Obviously, she hadn't thought far enough in advance. The sound of pounding feet on the hard, red dirt prevented her from replaying the past. It was the present that counted, the mission to save her brother and his friends.

She peeked through the palm fronds and noted that the two approaching men didn't use the marked path at all. She'd follow their example when she headed out once again, not wanting to hit any other mines or hidden traps.

Breathing shallowly and slowly, she calmed her rapid heart rate enough so the sound of it pounding in her ears would subside. She needed to hear what the men said.

The two walked around the small crater created by the explosion. One even scratched his head in a "what the fuck happened" gesture. She choked back a laugh. They might look confused, but she wouldn't count on it. Even clueless people could shoot to kill.

Her Spanish was more than good enough to follow their conversation and what they said was revealing. They were some of the mercs hired by Reyo Trujo to kill the SSI team. And from what they said, the trap had *not* been sprung—they were waiting on someone. Possibly Trujo?

If her intel proved accurate, there was a team of at least twenty mercs in this jungle version of Purgatory. If she eliminated these two, then there would only be eighteen or so.

Should she take these two out? And if she did, how soon would they be missed? Did they check in face-to-face? Over communication devices like the military used? She looked between the palm fronds and saw nothing in their ears or on their vests. Maybe they used walkie-talkies? She didn't see anything like those, either. Face-to-face, then. Odds were in her favor that by the time their buddies missed them, she'd have the guys heading out. Disabling these two would improve the odds later if there were a firefight.

Shooting them was out of the question. First, because it would be cold-blooded murder and second, there would be too much noise. The sound of gunfire carried miles at this altitude.

Could she overpower them and tie them up? She assessed the two men. On the plus side, they were short and wiry. On the negative side, they were mercs and probably had some military training.

She laughed silently. She also had military training. Growing up, she'd survived fights with five older brothers and all their friends. Then there were the attacks by predatory men and other assorted bad guys her brothers knew nothing about. The odds were better than good she could come out on top. But still, it would be better to take them one at a time.

And if she had to kill in self-defense, she always had her knife—the silent option.

She unbuttoned the shirt she'd just put on and stuffed it into her pack. Her tank top displayed a healthy amount of cleavage and some really nasty bruises and teeth marks. Maybe she could lure them over with sex and sympathy? She snorted. It was much more likely they'd see her as an easy victim with whom to wile away their afternoon. Either way, she was bait for the trap.

She let out a low moan and remained behind the pile of rubble. They could come to her.

"*¿Quién está allí?*" one of the men called out. Slowly, he headed in her general direction. She moaned again and he corrected his trajectory. He gestured to the other man to stay and guard.

"That's good, boys," she muttered, "investigate one at a time."

The man left behind nodded to his friend, his gaze quartering the area, maybe looking for a trap. She grinned. He was looking in all the wrong places.

His buddy walked toward her, also keeping an eye out.

She had to give them credit—they were cautious—but it wouldn't help them.

When the man spotted her, he froze in his tracks and let his gun's barrel drop toward the ground. *Big mistake, amigo.* A wide, leering smile broke out on his swarthy face. Bastard probably thought he'd died and gone to nookie heaven. Men—and Latino men especially—loved her pale cream-colored skin, her strawberry blonde curly hair, the full breasts on her petite frame. Suckers never looked to see it was all window dressing. Never noticed the muscles under all the female attributes or the calculating and sometimes lethal look in her eye.

The man opened his mouth to say something—to her or his friend—she didn't know or care. Smiling as if she were happy to see him, she moved toward him quickly, thrusting the heel of her hand up his nose, breaking it. He moaned and tried to turn away. Before he could attempt to shout to his friend or even defend himself, she chopped his windpipe sharply with the side of her hand and then grabbed his shoulders to steady him for a knee to his balls. As he bent over, bleeding, choking and gasping, she steadied him once more and thrust her knee forcefully into his diaphragm twice, effectively cutting off his ability to gain enough breath to make any loud noises for some time. Dirty fighting, but effective—and it all had taken less than fifteen seconds.

He fell to the ground like a stone, clutching his manhood and struggling to breathe. She pulled a set of flex-cuffs from her pocket, secured his hands behind his back and used his belt to bind his ankles. Pulling his shirt from his trousers, she used her knife and cut off a strip to gag him. He could breathe through his nose—just—so he wasn't in any danger of suffocating any time soon.

Keely then moved back under cover and waited for his friend to come find him. If the men had any communication devices, now would be the time for the other guy to use one. He didn't. Instead he called out, *"Pablo, ¿qué se está encendiendo?"* Too bad Pablo couldn't tell him what was going on.

Checking the area around him once more, Pablo's buddy headed her way. His finger was on the trigger of the semi-automatic weapon. Not good. She'd have to disable him before he could shoot. She pulled her knife and waited to take her best throw. If she failed, she'd resort to her handgun.

When the mercenary was ten feet away, she rose and threw the knife, hitting him in the arm. The knife stuck in his arm, just above his elbow. His finger slipped from the trigger as he grabbed to pull the knife out. She made her move and took him down just as she had Pablo. While he gasped for breath, she restrained him in the same manner as she had his friend. She retrieved her blade from his arm and cut his shirt for a compression bandage and a gag, then wiped the knife off on some grass and sheathed it.

She studied the two men who flopped on the ground like beached whales. She was in no immediate danger from them, but it was always possible if left apart that one might be flexible enough to escape the restraints and get away to warn the other mercs. She couldn't chance it.

Taking a page out of her father's "subduing the enemy" lecture, she tugged the two men closer together. God, they were heavier than they looked. She wiped the sweat dripping down her face with the hem of her tank top exposing her stomach and the lower curves of her breasts. Pablo stilled his frantic movements, his leering gaze fixed on her exposed skin.

"Pervert," she muttered. She pulled out her last set of flex-cuffs and secured the men to each other, back-to-back by their bound hands. Both men made noises around their gags. She was pretty sure her ancestors and her were receiving a tongue-lashing in Spanish. She patted each of them on the head. "Save your breath, *amigos.* You might just live long enough for someone to rescue you."

She retrieved her pack, pulled out some duct tape and wrapped their lower legs together and secured the cloth gags by covering them with the multi-purpose tape. They weren't going anywhere. They were close enough to the main path some villager would see them sooner or later and let them go. She wasn't going to worry about it. Old Pablo would have raped her in an instant, then turned her over to his friend. She'd seen it in his cold black eyes.

Stripping them of their extra ammunition, she put it in her backpack. After shrugging her shirt back on, she picked up her pack and put it on, shouldered one of the downed men's weapons and kept the other in her hand, ready to fire. Tweeter and the guys might need the extra weapons and ammunition if they had to fight their way back to the chopper.

Checking out the submachine guns, she said, "Hmm, H&K MP5. Very nice, boys. And clean. My dad always did say 'Keely, take care of your weapon and it will take care of you.' Too bad you had to run across me on one of my mean days."

The men glared at her, making noises in the backs of their throat. She turned away from them and resumed her trek to the village, paralleling the path but staying off it. Looking back, she made sure the men couldn't be seen too easily from the path. They couldn't. The undergrowth was too thick.

Using more caution than before, she stealthily approached the village. The meeting the SSI team was to attend was to be held at the local version of a cantina.

She stopped on the outskirts of the village, although calling it a village was generous. There were three small palapas, typical rain forest huts woven out of palm leaves, and one larger, sturdier building, the bottom half of which was constructed of local wood with a roof of tightly woven leaves.

If she were a betting woman, she'd put her money on the larger building being the bar. It had a generator running outside of it, meaning there could be cold beverages inside. The thought of anything cold and wet right now sounded orgasmic. She swiped a sweaty curl that had escaped her hat out of her eyes.

Sidling around the edge of the village, still under the cover of the forest, she moved until she was immediately behind the cantina. She'd seen no one. No villagers. No mercs. That worried her. Had those two bozos been wrong? Had the trap been sprung while the two had a siesta? Where were the sentries? Or were the bad guys all holed up somewhere, waiting on *el jefe*?

She crossed a small clearing and crept toward a hole serving as a window on the side of the building. The noise of the nearby generator would cover any sounds she might make. Letting out a breath, she peeked over the sill of the opening.

Her shoulders sunk in relief. Tweeter was in there. Alive. Safe—for now.

She also spotted Renfrew Maddox. A frisson of awareness shot down her spine at seeing him in the flesh. He was huge, even sitting down. His face was all angles, his jaw stubbled with a day or more of growth. His dark hair was longer than it had been in the military photo she'd seen in the DoD file she'd downloaded. His eyes were grey-blue like those of an Arctic wolf—and like the wolf he looked to be a predator. He reminded her of the men in her family—all male, all macho—and all deadly grace.

The other SSI operative was the Russian, no, he was Ukrainian, Vanko Petriv. His icy blond good looks and slightly smaller stature when compared to Maddox and her brother was deceptive—and she imagined a lot of his opponents had underestimated him to their detriment. The file she had on him described his training as an assassin. He'd often gone under deep cover for Interpol to ferret out Russian *mafiya* terrorizing European enterprises.

She scanned the room again to see who else was present. That was all of them—other than the bartender.

God, Maddox had balls. She shook her head. That or he was stump-stupid, only bringing three men to an intel meeting supposedly on al Qaeda operations in the Triple Frontier. But Maddox had been a highly decorated SEAL and Petriv had his lethal reputation through Interpol. Plus, her brother wasn't exactly helpless either. While he had a doctorate and never served in the military, he had the advantage of being trained by their dad and beat on by four older brothers. She smiled. She called Tweeter an alpha-geek, a nerd with muscles. So, maybe it only took three SSI operatives to deal with a meet. And, of course, they hadn't known their intel gathering mission was a death trap designed specifically for Maddox.

Ghosting along the side of the building toward the back, she stopped before inching around the corner. Good thing, too. An armed man came out of the dense rain forest foliage, striding toward the rear entrance of the bar in an "I'm-the-king-of-the-jungle" manner.

He must have seen her movement because he quickly headed her way. When he saw her fully, his jaw dropped open. He recovered instantly. This guy was more by-the-book, not as lecherous or easily distracted by a woman as Pablo. He raised his weapon and opened his mouth to yell at or challenge her. His demeanor was fierce, mean—and deadly. He was twice her size. He looked buff and strong. No time to take him out hand-to-hand, if she even could.

Her assessment of the situation had taken less than two seconds. In even less time, she pulled her knife and in one fluid movement, threw it. She caught him in the throat, cutting off anything he might have yelled. She hurried to meet him as he stumbled around. The man didn't know it yet but he was dead. Still, he grabbed at the knife with both hands, his gun falling to the ground. His expression was shocked as he stared at her. He grew weak quickly. His mouth opened and closed like a guppy seeking air. His eyes dimmed as life drained out of him.

Pushing aside pity, she stiff-armed him with her left arm, then pulled the knife from his throat with her right hand. Blood gushed from the wound, but it was not arterial. He would take a while to die and suffer horrific pain. She had to finish him off and warn her brother about the imminent attack. This man had been the advance man. She had no doubt in her mind they'd have to fight their way out now. She'd beaten the main attack, maybe by minutes.

Taking a deep breath, she murmured a silent prayer before slicing him across his carotid, using a backhanded motion. She danced away from the arterial spray as the man fell to the ground. His lifeless eyes turned to the sky.

Keely turned her head and gagged. Pulling her canteen from her pack, she drank, swallowing the sickness threatening to rise in her throat once more. She wiped the knife on a tussock of grass by the building before sheathing it.

How much time did they have? She stared into the dense green foliage. She saw nothing. The sounds of the rain forest were loud, seemed normal, so no one approached yet. Her gut told her they might have ten, maybe fifteen minutes.

She picked up the dead man's gun from where he'd dropped it, another H&K. She drew the line at wading through the blood pooling around the man's body to retrieve his extra ammo. Turning, she approached the rear of the cantina, listing in her head what needed to be done. Clear the backroom. Secure it against intruders. Disable the bartender. She was on what she suspected to be a short clock, so she'd better get to it. Aftermath for the bloody kill could come later—much later, at the hotel.

Sticking her head around the doorframe, she found no one in the crammed-to-the-rafters back room. It wasn't big and there were no places to hide. She entered, then shut the door and slid a metal bar used to lock it through an iron loop. That should slow down anyone trying to sneak in the back. Just in case, she quietly shifted a couple of cases of empty beer bottles in front of the door. Breaking bottles would make a lot of noise, warning them.

Now for the barkeep. She turned, then opened the door between the back room and the bar area. She thanked God someone kept the door hinges oiled. It barely made a sound. Looking around the corner, she located the room's four inhabitants. The bartender was behind the bar, and her brother, Maddox and Petriv were still at a table by the front door.

The bartender fidgeted, his body swaying from foot to foot, his gaze shifting to the doorway where she hid in the shadows. *Sorry, Charlie. Your buddy ain't coming to tell you what to do.*

As the bartender, his back to her now, began making what looked like a Mojito—lime, yummy—she ghosted into the room and came up behind him. She placed the flat blade of her less-than-pristine knife along the man's carotid.

"Don't move, *senor*. I might slip and cut you," she said, her voice loud enough to draw her brother and his team's attention. "Don't bother to finish the Mojito. We're not staying for drinks. Although I'd kill for a to-go Pepsi."

"Imp! What the fuck are you doing here?" Her brother's question was in the form of a roar. "And whose fucking blood is that?"

She glanced down and noted the blood spatter on her white shirt. Well, hell, she bet she had blood all over her face. *Eeuw.* She breathed slowly to dampen her renewed queasiness. No time to be sick, things would go tango uniform soon enough.

"No time for explanations. Someone needs to cover the door and windows. Company's coming." Using her knife as incentive, she forced the bartender to move with her—or chance getting his throat cut.

"Keely Ann Walsh!" Her brother stomped toward the bar. His face, a mask of calm, but his eyes held a powerful mixture of emotions—fear, concern, anger—all aimed at her. "Talk. Now."

Maddox followed her brother. Petriv moved to the side of the open doorway. At least someone was taking her seriously. "I was looking for you—to warn you." Her hand trembled; she really needed some sugar and fast. She wasn't kidding about killing for a Pepsi. She recognized now her nausea, her weakness was because she had low blood sugar, not an uncommon occurrence for her in hot, humid environments. The bartender jerked away from the blade. She pulled him back, emphasizing her point by pricking him with the point of her knife. "Not a good idea, *senor.*"

"About the company. Got that. Goddamit, are you hurt?" She recognized that tone. He wanted answers and he'd keep them there all the damn day until he got them.

She sighed. "It's not my blood, okay? Had a run-in with a merc out back."

Cursing in gutter Spanish, the bartender attempted to pull away again. She drew a line on the barkeep's flushed neck with the dull edge of her knife, leaving a trail of his friend's blood in the sweaty folds of fat. "Your friend is dead, *senor.* Please don't do anything stupid. I've done more than enough killing in the last two days."

The bartender spit to the side. "I have no friend, *senorita.* I am sorry, I also have no Pepsi. I have Coca-cola." His English had a Brooklyn-tinge to it.

The bartender tensed. Stupid, stupid. He was thinking, planning. She could almost see the wheels spinning in his head, powered by little Chihuahuas. She'd let it play out, see how dumb the man really was. Plus, the resulting lesson would show Tweeter's friends she could handle herself. They'd soon have to trust her to fight alongside them.

"Coke? That'll do." She withdrew the knife, giving the bartender an opening to make his move. "Get me one. Carefully."

Tweeter cursed under his breath. So did Maddox and Petriv, in assorted languages, each of them very vulgar. She shot them a warning glance. This was her fight, her lesson. Her brother glared at her and pointed his gun at the bartender's head. She shook her head and glared back. Overprotective brothers had been the bane of her existence. Maddox and Petriv she'd excuse for having their guns trained on the bartender, they didn't know any better. But Tweeter should. *Sheesh.*

Petriv moved away from the door to get another angle on the bartender's head. Maddox stood alongside her brother. The SSI owner's nostrils flared. His lips thinned. His piercing gaze watched every move she and the bartender made. Her conclusion? He was way pissed, but still ready to make a move to save her poor little female butt. She almost snorted. He'd learn she could save her own hind end—and soon. The bartender really was that stupid and would try to take her.

"A Coke for the *senorita. Un segundo.*" The man turned to smile at her. His face showed his shock. She got that a lot from men she'd held at knifepoint. The bartender's grin widened. Sucker thought he could take little ole her. *Not going to happen, dumbass.*

She sensed movement from her brother and Renfrew Maddox. She didn't shift her gaze away from the bartender as he reached toward an under-bar refrigerator. "Let the man get me my Coke, guys."

Maddox made a noise that sounded suspiciously like a growl.

"Keely—" The warning in her brother's voice would normally make her cringe, but she was too busy concentrating on the barkeep's movements. All weakness was temporarily gone, due to a timely surge of adrenaline. She fondled her knife, keeping it ready.

Instead of bending down to get a cold soda, the man turned, his head and body just enough below the bar top to mess up the other three's shots. He used his arm to knock her knife hand up and away. Expecting something like this, she kept a firm grip on her weapon. She thrust the heel of her left hand up and broke his nose. Too bad for *el fatso*—she had two hands and was equally adept with both.

There was still some fight in the man. Howling, he lunged for her. Using his forward momentum, she blocked the hand reaching for her knife with her forearm and kneed him in the balls. Then to add insult to injury, she used the old trusty knee to the diaphragm. Her dad and brothers had taught her to fight dirty. While the big strong man thought he could contain the little slip of a female, she had him on the ground, crying like a little girl.

By the time Tweetie and Maddox came around the bar, she'd flipped the very unhappy barkeep and had a booted foot in the small of his back, holding him down, her knifepoint at the nape of his neck.

"You got any flex-cuffs? I used mine on the way here. My source in Puerto Iguazu only had three sets. I was just thrilled the guy had ordnance for the Kamov that'll haul our butts out of here."

Her brother's lips thinned and flags of white appeared around them. His was furious, but containing it well. After all, he *was* the most even-tempered of her brothers. He tossed her a set of cuffs from his belt, which she caught with her left hand. Pressing down on the bartender's left kidney with the heel of her hiking boot, she sheathed her knife and cuffed the man's hands behind his back, then flipped him over. His moan told her she might have broken a rib or two. She blamed it on the adrenaline.

Now that the immediate danger was past, she was shaking from the combination of too much adrenaline and too little sugar. Stepping over the downed man, she peered in the refrigerator under the bar and indeed found cold, six-ounce bottles of Coke. Pulling out two of the small bottles, she closed the door. Popping the top off one on the edge of the counter, she held up a finger toward her brother who had relaxed enough to open his mouth to speak, then downed one bottle. God, she needed that. She could already feel the sugar and caffeine blasting into her bloodstream.

Maddox stood next to Tweeter, glancing from her to the man on the ground and back, a look of stunned disbelief on his chiseled face. Petriv joined the other two; his lips quirked. The stone-cold assassin was fighting a smile. Who knew he'd have a sense of humor? His file hadn't mentioned it. Intelligence files usually mentioned everything right down to the size of a man's dick. Petriv's was seven inches, slightly above average from all her reading; Maddox's, eight. She managed to avoid looking at their crotches to see if her intel had been correct.

Petriv caught her eye and winked at her. She inclined her head graciously. The Ukrainian threw back his head and laughed. Maddox shot Petriv an angry glare. Ooh, he didn't like his associate flirting with her, huh? Tweetie had told her his boss had no use for women and had established a "no-single-women-on-Sanctuary rule." Only operatives' wives, long-term, live-in girlfriends and fiancées were allowed to live on the property. The DoD and CIA files on Maddox labeled him as a loner; he'd had only two long-term relationships in his life, one for twelve months and another for nine, and neither of those women had lived with him 24/7. Knowing the male of the species fairly well—with a dad and five brothers how could she not?—he probably didn't avoid sexual conquests; he wasn't a monk, he just had no use for permanent relationships.

She placed the empty bottle on the bar with a thunk and opened the second. This one she intended to savor. "Uh, someone really needs to watch the door." She broke what had become an uncomfortable silence. She hated being the cynosure of everyone's eyes. "You were led into a trap, guys. I took care of the back door. The sound of breaking beer bottles means they're coming in that way."

"Keely, what the fuck…"

"Tweeter, you can't say that word. I'll tell Mom." Their mother, Molly Walsh, disliked the f-word, but with a house full of military men, she fought a losing battle. Her response was to demand payment—a quarter for every f-bomb. Her mother sported some very nice jewelry because the Walsh men and their friends uttered a lot of f-words.

Keely frowned at her brother to underline her point, then turned to the man at his side and held out her hand.

"Mr. Maddox? In case you hadn't guessed, I'm his little sister. I worked on a project for NSA through the auspices of my employer MIT until about twenty hours ago. While working for them, I came across this anomaly in the COMINT, uh, the communications intelligence I processed—which I will explain later if y'all really want to know the deets. Bottom line, this is a trap. There is no al Qaeda cell in this hole in the jungle. They're all across the river in Paraguay, if you really want to know. *This* is a trap set by Reyo Trujo, who seems to have a humongous hard-on for you, through the machinations of a highly placed traitor in the Department of Defense." Then she smiled sweetly and pulled out a granola bar from her pocket, unwrapped it and took a bite. Caffeine and sugar only went so far in combating low blood sugar—and she'd need all the energy she could muster for the fight to come.

Maddox looked at her hands as if they might rear up and bite him. Again a sound somewhere between a rumble and a snarl came from deep in his chest. His icy grey-blue eyes warmed and turned a deep, smoky slate blue. His gaze traveled over her as if trying to classify her species—or figuring where to take a bite out of her first. She shivered. Now, she knew firsthand what a soft furry bunny felt like when a wolf had it in its sights. The man was an honorable, dominant, alpha male with predatory tendencies, much like her dad and brothers. This was a good news-bad news thing. Good in that she knew how to deal with the alpha personality; bad in that such honorable alphas wanted to cocoon her in bubble wrap and put her somewhere safe.

She didn't get "put" easily.

"Keely." Tweeter's voice had gone low and soft. Too soft. He was pissed—and really, really scared. "How did you get here?"

When in doubt about handling men getting on their protective high-horses, her mom told her to answer their questions literally, in great detail and at length. Such responses had a way of distracting the overprotective male.

"I flew commercial until Puerto Iguazu—and let me tell you there are no straight-through flights anywhere in this part of the world."

Someone snorted. She turned. Had the sound, much like stifled laughter, come from Maddox? Nah, his face was stone cold, the expression of a man who ate nails for breakfast. She must have imagined the sound. He caught her look and raised an arrogant dark brow. She glared at him, then turned back to her brother.

"Then I rented a chopper—"

"The Kamov," Petriv offered. He winked at her. Again. A trained assassin with a sense of the ridiculous. How fun. "A good bird."

She shot him a sunny smile. "Yes—you were listening. Good, 'cause we need to get out of here." She chased the granola with the second Coke, then stepped over the wiggling bartender and headed around the bar.

None of the three men moved. She stood, hands on her hips. "Did y'all hear me? Bad guys. Twenty of them or maybe more—well, come to think of it, seventeen or maybe more … I'm not counting the bartender—are coming to kill you."

Her brother grabbed her arms and shook her. She winced. "Tweets, you don't know your strength. You're hurting me."

He hovered over her, attempting to use his foot or so advantage in height to intimidate her. He should have learned by now it didn't work on her, but he always tried.

"Don't give me that crap," he said, exasperation in his voice. "I'm hardly touching you. Are you sure none of this is your blood?" His forehead creased with concern as his gaze traveled her torso and a finger traced the blood spatter down the front of her shirt.

She slapped his hand away, then leaned her forehead on his chest and sighed. Unwanted tears welled in her eyes. She refused to let them fall. That was a wussy-assed thing to do, and there was no time to be weak. She was safe and her brother was safe. She'd made it in time.

He held her more tightly against him. "I hate to ask—but why are there now only seventeen or so mercs left?" He took her hat off and leaned his chin on top of her disheveled, sweaty curls, his fingers soothing her scalp as he untangled the mess now falling to the center of her back.

One of the other two men gasped. Typical male response to her hair. She hated her hair. Most days, it was a nuisance. It was thick and heavy, and in hot humid weather, it curled and frizzed like crazy. But all her brothers, her dad and, most importantly, her mama begged her not to cut it.

"Why seventeen, Keely Ann Walsh?" He rocked her within the circle of his arms as he used to do when she skinned her knees as a little girl.

"Because I had to, um, disable two on the way here and then kill the guy out back. I was on a short clock, like Dad always says. I couldn't let anyone or anything stop me from getting here. Okay?" She wasn't happy that her last word had ended on a shrill note. She took a breath and let it out slowly. If she had a mantra, she'd be chanting it.

"Okay, calm down, Imp." He smoothed her hair, a losing battle since it always did what it wanted to anyway. "Did you see any of the other mercs?"

"Nope, but I think the guy who I killed out back was coming to let the bartender know the attack was imminent. The two guys on the trail said something about waiting on someone. I figured Trujo wanted to be in on the kill."

Maddox grunted, drawing her attention. As he opened his mouth to say something, probably something macho and sexist, several rounds of automatic gunfire hit the front of the building, burning through the flimsy wood like a knife through butter. The mirror behind the bar shattered under the barrage, showering her and Tweeter with glass.

She shoved out of Tweeter's arms then pulled him to the floor. Satisfied he hadn't been hit, she belly-crawled from behind the bar, ignoring everything but the need to get to the back room to retrieve the H&Ks she'd left there along with her backpack and all the ammo.

"Keely," Tweeter yelled, his hand just slipping off her booted foot.

"I've got her," Maddox shouted. "Start laying down some fire out the front and block the fucking door!"

Continuing her fast crawl, she threw a frowning glance over her shoulder. "Has my mom met you?" He shook his head, confusion evident in his eyes. "Don't ever use the f-bomb around her. She'll make you pay."

Maddox snorted. Same sound she'd heard earlier. He'd been—still was—laughing at her. *Ass.*

"You think that's funny? Just wait until you owe her a small fortune," Keely muttered.

He put a large hand on her hips, shoving gently. "Move it. What have you got in the back room? An arsenal?"

"How'd you guess?" She ignored his sarcastic tone and threw a glare over her shoulder. "Move the hand. Tweetie is looking—and he won't like it."

He slowly pulled his hand away, caressing her rear end. "Tweetie?"

They were in the middle of a fight for their lives and he wanted to share personal family info? Fine. She could multi-task. "I couldn't say Tweeter when I was little. Want to know when my brothers first short-sheeted my bed?"

He grinned and shook his head. "Maybe later."

He choked back another laugh at her muttered, "Ass." She dragged the backpack to her and pulled out ammo, tossing him a couple of magazines and then one of the H&Ks.

His mouth quirked. "Hand me the extra H&K for the guys. They'll need the extra firepower." He stuck his hand out.

She shoved the weapon at him, which he took and crawled into the other room. He'd left his weapon so he was obviously coming back. Lucky her.

Out of habit, she checked it over for him. Say what you would about hired guns, they did take care of their weapons. The H&K was clean and good to go.

After shoving some boxes of canned foods around, she built a place for them to hide behind. She put bags of flour in front of the boxes. Might stop some bullets from getting through. Then she dropped behind the makeshift barricade and checked her weapon again. Maddox crawled back into the room and gave her preparations a surprised and approving look. She answered the unasked question in his eyes. "Too many years of following my brothers around and playing war games." She shoved his gun toward him. "I checked it. Thirty-round mags and I set it for bursts."

"Trained by a Marine, I see." He checked over the weapon himself.

She wasn't insulted. He'd be dumb if he hadn't. "My dad—and a couple of SEALs. My oldest two brothers are Navy." She wished they were here now. It sounded like WWIII in the front. She anticipated an attack on the back any time.

Before Maddox could make a comment, something thudded against the back door. Two more thuds and the bad guys figured they couldn't knock it down, so they shot at it. Splinters flew as the door was riddled with bullets.

Keely lay on her stomach and poked the muzzle of her weapon through a firing hole she'd created. Maddox was next to her, his body heat and male scent engulfing her. She felt more threatened by his closeness than by the murderous goons attempting to breach the back door. She wiggled away, opening up her personal space, but he followed, his body now touched her from hip to ankle. *Damn.* He was ready to cover her body with his to protect her. He'd learn eventually—she always carried her weight. She didn't need a man to cover her ass.

He looked at her. "Short bursts. Go for the head. They might have body armor." He followed his words with an example, aiming head high through the door. A body fell through the decimated door. A perfect head shot.

She shouted to be heard over the return fire. "I know. Don't baby me. I can hit what I aim for. You could ask my brother, but he and Petriv sound busy."

The merc force had thrown the main firepower to the front. Maybe they thought the SSI men would be distracted and forget there was a back door. That would be stupid thinking on the mercs' part. She let off a short burst of gunfire at the next man who stuck his head around the shredded door. The man fell forward on top of his buddy, the top of his head missing.

Keely touched Maddox's muscled, hairy forearm. His arm tensed under her fingers. His eyes burned blue like the heart of a gas flame as he turned to look at her. She frowned— distracted by the flames in his eyes. He wasn't angry, but she wasn't sure what he was feeling. She shook off the effect of his intent look. "Um, FYI, the three I took out had no armor. It's too frick-fracking hot for Kevlar."

Maddox laughed, a full-out sound that reached into her gut and turned her insides to mush. O-o-kay, the guy could lighten up—though now might not be the right time.

While the battle raged at the front of the building, the gunfire had temporarily halted at their position. The enemy had to reassess their strategy. Two of theirs were down and they hadn't even fully breached the rear of the cantina. The lull would not last forever. Already, Keely's neck itched like crazy. It would be soon.

"Way too hot." He lifted her chin with a calloused finger. This time she was the one to tense. She had the little-prey-feeling again. She licked suddenly dry lips, wishing for another Coke. His gaze turned frigid, the color of Arctic ice. "No one gets through."

In other words, don't be a girl about killing. If he only knew— "Gotcha." She attempted to smile, but failed. "Don't worry, Mr. Maddox."

"It's Ren." He tweaked her chin. "Say it."

The cessation of fire at their position still held, but it couldn't be much longer before someone tested the door again. *Humor the man, Keely.* "Ren."

His eyes warmed. She licked her lips again. His eyes darkened to the deep grey-blue color peculiarly his before he turned away to concentrate on the rear entrance. Yet, she sensed he knew every breath she took, every movement she made, even if it was minor.

"Uh, I won't let y'all down." She bit her lower lip. "I just wish I could've warned you before you left Idaho. Some guy named Quinn said I just missed Tweetie."

"You made good time. We just got here two hours ago."

She fixed her gaze on the door and away from him. He was a distraction—and she was usually hard to distract. She focused on her weapon, her finger ready to pull the trigger. "You had to sneak in. I came direct. Makes a difference." She took a deep breath. "They're regrouping—it shouldn't be long now."

"Yeah. Nervous?"

She caught his sideways glance. He was concerned. He probably wished her anywhere but here. His type would always protect the little helpless woman. She wished she could convince him she could handle her end of the fight. Well, he'd learn soon enough. "A little. I hate killing. But I'll do what I have to do."

"But you shouldn't the fuck have to." His tone was angry tinged with regret.

"I tried to get some of my brothers freed up, but they would have been too late."

His look told her she should've tried harder. She was tempted to stick her tongue out at him, but just then his head whipped around to face forward as two men burst into the room through the decimated wood door. Their guns blazed amidst the crash of bottles as the cases spilled open. The two were immediately followed by others. *Guess the strategy was to hit them all at once.*

In her shooting zone, Keely was barely aware of anything around her. She shot in short bursts, aiming for heads and legs. When it became evident that they did not, in fact, have body armor, she adjusted and went for heart shots, even if she missed the heart, torso shots at this caliber had stopping power. Her mathematical mind figured angles and trajectories, anticipated movements and coordinated with her muscle movement and eye-to-hand coordination. Her sniper training courtesy of one of her dad's buddies stood her well. She wasted no ammunition. Each man she aimed at, she hit. When they went down, they stayed down.

She emptied a magazine and swiftly and efficiently ejected it and inserted another.

Ren's muttered "goddamn—a warrior sprite" had her glancing his way. But he was concentrating on shooting and not her. She must have imagined his words.

They fell into a rhythm, each taking out every other man through the narrow door. When one reloaded, the other took up the slack. It was as if they could read each other's minds.

Finally, the attackers stopped coming. Bodies lay strewn across the floor of the small back room. Smoke hung in the air. Silence fell over the bullet-riddled building. Tweeter and Petriv spoke in low rumbles in the other room. But Keely's tension increased rather than decreased with the cessation of the attack.

"Fudge ripple, that's not good. It was too easy." She looked at Ren. His eyes were narrowed as he examined her. "I don't like this. Maybe my intel wasn't complete. There were too many of them—so there could be a lot more out there."

"They could've changed the plan after you set out." Ren's tone was low, rumbling, meant to soothe her. "Don't worry about it, sprite."

She hadn't imagined him calling her that earlier. Before she could call him on the carpet— "Something's coming."

"What?" Ren turned toward her, crowding into her personal space even more. "What do you…"

A grenade thrown through the doorway tumbled into the room.

Ren's "fuck" barely registered. Keely was closer. Tossing her weapon to the side, she went for the explosive. As she rolled across the floor toward another set of boxes, she grabbed the live grenade, then lobbed it side-handed out the rear door. She kept rolling and made it behind some boxes of frijoles before the explosion rocked the back of the building.

She rolled onto her stomach and pulled her Bren from the holster at her back. She flicked off the safety and held it two-handed just in case someone was alive to follow through.

"Keely, what the fuck was that?" Her brother's frightened bellow was loud and cut through the ringing in her ears. She could make out Petriv swearing in some highly colorful Russian.

A quick glance told her Ren was okay—but visibly furious. "Don't you ever fucking do that again!" He glared at her instead of paying attention to the new hole in the wall.

She shrugged and fired over his head at a man attempting to come through the smoldering opening. The dead man drooped over the jagged remnants of the wall, half in and half out of the room.

After another furious glance at her, Ren double-tapped the intruder to make sure he was dead.

Why the heck was he mad at her? She'd kept them from being blown into hamburger and then saved his life? She deserved an "atta-girl."

Silence reigned once more over the small, battered building. Her itchy feeling was gone, thank the Lord. She laid her weary head on her forearms, but kept her handgun in her right hand, just in case her spider sense was wrong.

"Keely!" Tweeter's worried voice came from the front room once more.

"I'm fine, Tweetie. How many did you get on your side?"

"Vanko and I got us a confirmed ten motherfuckers."

She ignored her brother's profanity, allowing for the situation. "My three on the way here plus your ten plus we have eleven, no, make that twelve on the floor and hanging over the hole in the wall. That's twenty-five. We might have taken out one or two with the grenade out the back door…"

"What fucking grenade?" Tweeter yelled. "Where did you get a fucking grenade?'

"The live grenade your fool sister picked up and threw out the back door." Ren's jaw clenched and unclenched. He belly crawled toward her.

"Tattletale." She stuck out her tongue.

His eyes narrowed as he moved toward her. "Brat."

Ignoring him, she turned and crawled into the bar area with Ren so close behind her she could feel his hot breath on the bare skin of her legs above her hiking boots. She met her brother just inside the doorway as he crab-walked toward her. He looked her over, then sighed.

"I think that's the same blood you already had." He closed his eyes and shook his head. "Imp, don't do that shit. Let us do it."

"It" being the throwing of live grenades, she supposed. "*It* was closer to me—and I know how to handle a live grenade, ya know." And why was she getting defensive?

"Yeah, Mom never let Dad live that training session down, did she?" He grinned at her. A shaky finger stroked her cheek.

"Nope, she didn't." She sat up and pulled her knees to her chest, her arms hanging loosely over her bent knees, her gun still in her right hand. "There could be more mercs waiting in the jungle—or the survivors of this team could be regrouping. I say we get out of here before they can come at us with bigger guns or something. Plus, we have the belly guns on the helo and all that armor-plating Russians love to layer on their aircraft. I'll feel better once we're up and can shoot down on them."

Petriv's shout of laughter had her smiling. Someone appreciated her. She grinned at the Ukrainian.

Knee-walking, Ren came up against her back. His knee nudged her bottom and his body almost covered hers from behind. He grabbed her arms, keeping her from moving away from his heat and scent. What was his problem now? She was just sitting here.

"Ren?" Tweeter frowned. "You're crowding my baby sister. Back off."

About the Author

A Hoosier born and raised, Monette still lives in the heartland near Indianapolis, Indiana. Married to her college sweetheart and soul mate, she has one son.

After many years of practicing law, Monette found that all the clients, opposing counsel, and the problems she handled ignited the need to write fiction. So she started writing – first, romantic suspense/thrillers, then adding a touch of paranormal and scifi and, eventually, a sexier side (as Rae Morgan).

Monette (and Rae) loves to hear from her fans. E-mail her at monettemichaels@gmail.com.

VISIT HER AT:

www.monettemichaels.com

- authormonettemichaels
- MonetteMichaels
- monettemichaels

Author Bibliography

Writing as Monette Michaels:

Fatal Vision

Death Benefits

Green Fire

Vested Interests

Blind-Sided (with Janet Ferran)

The Virtuous Vampire,
A Gooden and Knight Mystery, Case File #1

The Deadly Séance,
A Gooden and Knight Mystery, Case File #2

Eye of the Storm,
Book 1, Security Specialists International

Stormy Weather Baby,
Book 1.5, Security Specialists International

Cold Day in Hell,
Book 2, Security Specialists International

Storm Front,
Book 2.5, Security Specialists International

Weather the Storm,
Book 3, Security Specialists International

Storm Warning,
Book 4, Security Specialists International

Prime Obsession,
Book 1, The Prime Chronicles Trilogy

Prime Selection,
Book 2, The Prime Chronicles Trilogy

Prime Imperative,
Book 3, The Prime Chronicles Trilogy

Prime Claiming,
a Prime Chronicles Short Story

WRITING AS RAE MORGAN:

DESTINY'S MAGICK,
BOOK 1, COVEN OF THE WOLF SERIES

MOON MAGICK,
BOOK 2, COVEN OF THE WOLF SERIES

TREADING THE LABYRINTH,
BOOK 3, COVEN OF THE WOLF SERIES

"NO SECRETS,"
BOOK 4, COVEN OF THE WOLF,
IN THE ZODIAC: PISCES ANTHOLOGY

EARTH AWAKENED,
A TERRAN REALM BOOK

ENCHANTRESS

"EVANESCENCE,"
IN THE EDGE OF NIGHT ANTHOLOGY

"ONCE UPON A PRINCESS,"
IN AIN'T YOUR MAMA'S BEDTIME STORIES